THE SUPREMACY LICENSE

A SINATRA THRILLER

ALAN LEE

SPARKLE PRESS

The Supremacy License
A Sinatra Thriller

by Alan Lee

Copyright © 2019 Alan Janney

First Edition
Printed in USA

Cover by Damonza
Formatting by Vellum
Paperback ISBN: 9781795456197

Sparkle Press

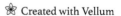 Created with Vellum

PROLOGUE

FBI Senior Special Agent Weaver sipped her Folgers instant coffee. She'd mixed the cup herself; it was weak and burnt and she winced. But she hadn't found any Starbucks open at this hour.

Next to her sat Douglas, the DEA's Director for Special Operations. His blocky face turned shades of blue as he browsed files on his iPad. Their flight landed half an hour ago, and he'd spent every minute since on the device. He looked a little like an ape jabbing at a toy.

The door opened and Noelle Beck walked into their small conference room. She placed a manila folder in front of each. The papers inside still warm.

"Thank you, Ms. Beck," said Senior Special Agent Weaver. "I know it's early."

"That's alright, ma'am. I'll be at my desk if you need me."

The young woman left, covering a yawn and closing the door.

Weaver and Douglas read through the identical files—exemplary performance evaluations, impressive track record; he outpaced the others three-to-one in apprehensions. But she knew all that. Nothing revelatory here.

In a rumbling voice, Douglas said, "Performance is good. Still the questions about insubordination. And excessive force."

Weaver smiled to herself. "That's not a red flag."

"Independent. Works alone."

"Perfect."

He said, "And the drug use?"

"His childhood was hell. Every other kid growing up like him is in prison or dead. He survived. I'd be suspicious if there *wasn't* drug use, including the occasional relapse. Army was a godsend at nineteen. Same for L.A.P.D. He's straight now. I work with men like him all day, every day—he's bored. He's still angry and broken. The job's a relief, but he hates the paperwork. Looking for a change. Again, perfect for me."

"You think he can keep it together."

"I do."

Douglas, still looking at the papers, asked, "Why."

"Here's a simplistic answer—the way he dresses. It's the sign of a well-ordered mind. Someone who brings discipline to everything he can."

Douglas snapped the file closed. "You've already made up your mind about him."

"It's just that, we have no choice."

THE SUPREMACY LICENSE

"You are right, Mr. Bond... All the greatest men are
maniacs."
-Ian Flemming, *Dr. No*

1

The sliding doors parted and Deputy US Marshal Martinez brought the cool morning into the lobby with him. He'd arrived at the office early, so out of character the security guard glanced at his watch to verify the time—7:20am. Most days the security guard had clocked out before Martinez arrived.

This was a treat. Martinez was his favorite.

He was everyone's favorite.

The Roanoke Marshal's Office was built into the second floor of the Poff Building off Franklin, one of those glass monolithic monstrosities with no character. The sentry ran Martinez's credentials at the checkpoint, a process aimed at logging personnel rather than at security.

The sentry said, "Looking sharp, Deputy Martinez. As usual."

"This is America, Tony. She's a country worth dressing up for."

"Yes sir." Tony suppressed a smile—Martinez knew his name without looking. "Lotta people here early today."

"In the Marshal's office?"

Tony nodded.

He said, "Two officials from Washington. They got in an hour ago. Don't know them. Their credentials cleared but wouldn't log."

Manny pinched at the bridge between his eyes and grimaced. He hoped the officials weren't here to hold meetings. He hated meetings.

"Next time, don't let them in."

"I'll try, sir." Before Martinez could leave, he added, "You haven't caught a terrorist yet today? You're slowing down."

"Got a drug dealer in my trunk, amigo. Saving him for later."

The sentry chuckled. He'd tell the others about the conversation. Everyone enjoyed a good Manny Martinez story. The deputy was joking about having a villain in his trunk, probably, but the great thing about him was that you couldn't know for sure.

Manny pressed his eyes against the retinal scanners at the second fire door and entered the inner sanctum.

The deputy marshals kept their desks in an open bullpen, surrounded by private conference rooms and utilitarian areas. The place felt hard and neat and ugly. Deputies didn't spend much time at their desks anyway. The walls gleamed with laminated posters—mandated safety warnings, federal policies, mugshots of fugitives.

Manny's desk was a work of art, luxury and steel buffed to a high shine. It wrapped around his Herman Miller Aeron swivel chair on three sides, giving him a full range of work space. Neither the desk nor the chair were government issue; he'd purchased them with personal funds and carted them in one weekend, bemusing his coworkers and irritating the marshal. Most others worked on drab particleboard affairs.

His desk pressed against Noelle Beck's, facing one another; their computer monitors almost touched. An NSA computer technician on six-month loan to the Marshal's Western Virginia District, she had four monitors arranged around her chair.

Manny twisted out of his tailored beige sports coat, slid into his Aeron chair, and activated the computer. The machine clicked and hummed to life. This early the office was quiet. He unclipped the Glock 27 from his belt and laid it in the top drawer.

Unseen beyond her monitor, Noelle Beck yawned and noted, "You're early."

"I skipped the gym. Paperwork to do."

"Paperwork? I thought you forgot."

"I don't forget." He pressed the heels of his hands into his eyes and sighed. An elongated and expressive blast of air. "I just hate it."

"I took—"

"I hate paperwork, Beck."

"But if you—"

"Haaaaaaaate it."

Beck's voice was warm and smiling. "Okay. Suit yourself."

Manny opened the government database software. His files should've been updated last night but had he been punctual with the paperwork he'd have missed cocktails at the Patrick Henry bar. He didn't care much about the marshal's wrath but lectures were best avoided.

He drummed his fingers, glaring hatefully. He said, "Beck."

"Yes Manuel?"

Manny winced. He hated her use of his full name. "I'm sorry for interrupting you earlier. That was rude. And I am never rude."

"Yes you are."

"I'm working on it."

On screen, his email opened and he zipped through the inbox. He needed to update the database—the very thought filled him with pain. Databases were straight from hell, so he permitted himself to sidetrack.

At precisely eight o'clock, Collin Parks strolled in with a mug of coffee. One of the ridiculous plastic mugs from Taiwan, leaking heat. Collin was short and compact with cauliflower ears, like he did well wrestling in high school and decided to keep the body. Brawn over brain.

Collin made a grunting noise. "Looking good, Mulder and Scully."

Manny didn't reply. He'd fallen deep into an email about luxury shirts from Barneys. And he'd never bothered to find out who Mulder and Scully were. A dashing duo, he assumed. Some days he fantasized about kicking Collin's ass.

Thirty minutes later Manny still lounged in his swivel chair, scrolling through an email about gang unrest due to Whitey Bulger's death and what it meant for government informants, when the marshal walked in.

Bert Warren, nicknamed The Bear—man looked like he could outwrestle a grizzly, even though Bert was in his sixties. He'd worked his way from an Army MP to FBI special agent to a Presidentially appointed marshal for the western half of Virginia. Never married, hard working, dependable, and well liked.

Warren made a beeline for Manny's desk.

He rumbled, "Morning, Ms. Beck."

"Good morning, Marshal."

He shoved a thick finger at Manny. "Just hung up with Sheriff Stackhouse. She says you brought in Milo Wiggins last night."

Manny stood and straightened his tie. "He come with a bonus?"

Across the room, Collin Parks set his plastic mug down hard enough to spill it. "Milo Wiggins?"

"Morning, Deputy Parks." Warren said it without looking at him.

"Shit." Collin grabbed at tissues to mop up the coffee. "Milo Wiggins, you kidding? He's mine."

Manny said, "Milo coming through Roanoke. I saw him last night and I cuffed him. Not a tough hombre."

"Milo was on *my* case load," said Collin.

"You're lazy. Took too long."

"And you knew he was coming through town."

"I knew."

"How?"

"I knew."

"You had Milo for a year, Parks," said Marshal Warren. "And you sat on it."

"Sat on it? Sir, he was out of state."

Manny shook his head. "You didn't look hard enough. You, the lazy communist. Me, hardworking American."

"You act like these guys fall into your lap, Manny. And it ain't that easy. You cheat."

Manny raised his hands, palms up. "I'm on the Fugitive Task Force. I ran into Milo. What's a poor Hispanic boy supposed to do?"

"Sheriff says Milo looks like hell," said Marshal Warren. "And Milo says you beat him up. That you let him go, then beat him up some more."

"Sounds like Milo is a lying fugitive, you ask me."

"He says you shot him."

"With *wax* bullets. They don't count."

Collin finished mopping his coffee and chucked the sodden paper towels into the trash can. With vigor. "All Manny's collars say the same thing. Those who live long enough to talk. They all claim he kicks the piss out of them."

"Milo Wiggins, he hurts women and children. He put up a fight when I respectfully asked him to get in the car. So I talked sense into him."

Behind the monitor, Beck snickered.

Marshal Warren's phone buzzed. He pulled it from his pocket and held it away from his face, reading the text. The font was sized large and he still had to squint.

"Milo's attorney will be here in thirty minutes," he said. "Hotshot from Washington. Thousand bucks an hour, politically connected. Milo's paperwork isn't perfect, we got a mess on our hands."

Manny nodded. Ah. The paperwork. Should've done that.

Warren's eyes hit with the force of a truck. "Tell me his workup is pristine, Deputy Martinez."

Manny adjusted his tie again. Cleared his throat. Yes, he thought. About the paperwork.

Noelle Beck stood. "Pristine, sir. Deputy Martinez spent hours on it last night. I assisted."

It was a lie. Manny suppressed his surprise. Mostly.

"Is that so." Marshal Warren alternated his glare between Manny and Noelle. She flinched each time. Handling Manny's paperwork was against the rules. Lying to the marshal would get her fired. And Warren knew when people were lying. "You assisted?"

"Yessir," said Noelle.

Manny made a note to buy Noelle Beck a bottle of champagne. Or a new car. Beck's work was always perfect and she saved his butt. She must've stayed an hour late.

"Pristine. Better be." Bert Warren dismissed it with a wave. Important matters pressed. He checked his watch. "Deputy Martinez, you have a meeting. Now. Then we meet with the attorney."

Manny half glanced toward his calendar laid on his desk. "Meeting? Not this morning."

"You do. The sheriff and I both signed off on the project."

The two officials from Washington. Top secret.

"What project?"

Warren looked him up and down. "The hell are you wearing?"

"Fashion."

From his desk, Collin said, "What, those pants are Gucci or something?"

"Gucci? I look like a fascist? This is American Trench. Cotton from the Carolinas. Maybe you need to look in the mirror more often, Parks."

"Be nice, one of these days, you showed up in uniform," said Marshal Warren.

Manny tucked his thumbs behind his belt. "You think uniforms capture desperados? Don't seem to work for Collin Parks. Maybe I put on the uniform, I start moving slower. Sir."

Warren beckoned him. "Follow please, Martinez."

"What is—"

Warren was already moving toward one of the private conference rooms in the distant corner.

Manny growled. He snatched his sports coat, circled

Noelle's desk, and whispered, "You are an angel from heaven, Noelle Beck, and I am in your debt."

"Don't make promises to a girl you won't keep."

"*Eres perfecta y te amo*," he said and she felt her cheeks burn. One reason she kept her computer monitor situated between them—so she could focus. She was good and she knew it and she was on her way up the NSA ladder. And ogling Manny didn't fit into her plans.

The funny thing was, the man seemed oblivious. He was proud of his fashion sense, his fitness, his discipline, but he couldn't care less about his face. And that was the best part.

2

Manny followed the marshal into the back. To one of the interrogation rooms, which surprised him. Two individuals waited at the stainless steel desk, a man and a woman, and they stood when he entered.

Bert Warren indicated him and said, "Special Agent, Director, meet Deputy Martinez."

The man and the woman shook Manny's hand. No names, no uniforms, but they wore the unmistakable stoicism of Mother Justice. Faces like shields, a no-nonsense preparedness.

The Director did not smile but he nodded his head. "Deputy Martinez, we need a few minutes of your time."

"Sure," said Manny. "You're a director? With the operations division?"

The man didn't answer.

The Special Agent said, "Marshal Warren, with your permission, we're going to speak with Deputy Martinez privately."

Marshal Warren expressed silent displeasure. He didn't enjoy being dismissed, and so quickly. This was his office after all. But he'd agree to the stipulations beforehand and his morning had filled. He snapped a nod and closed the door behind him, using more force than necessary.

Alone with the two senior officials, his curiosity piqued, Manny draped his jacket across the chair and they sat. The Special Agent noted the tattoos on Manny's forearm and she surreptitiously adjusted her stack of papers to get a second glance at his governmental headshot. The photograph didn't do him justice.

"For the sake of anonymity, our names aren't important. Not yet." The woman's brown hair was cut short. She had vibrant green eyes and an old scar running from temple to cheek. No wedding band. Manny guessed she'd been a Marine. "I'm a Senior Special Agent for the FBI and I direct the Joint Federal Investigations Commission. We're small. How small? I am the only full-time staffer for JFIC. No Christmas parties, no commemorative badges, no office potluck—we're lean and mean. I coordinate independent agents nationwide. Think of them as sleeper cells, ready to be activated for temporary assignment."

The large man cleared his throat. He was blocky with a buzz cut. He wore the suit of a career serviceman—plain black and two inches too big, a look Manny despised. Men should dress like men, not circus tents. "I'm here on behalf of a five-person oversight board, constituted by members from the DEA, the FBI, the CIA, the NSA, and the Federal Marshals."

The woman said, "We're here to discuss an assignment with you."

"You know about me," said Manny.

"We do. I cull a list of federal agents. You were at the top and suddenly you are needed."

"How many sleeper cells in JFIC?"

"Three. You'd be the fourth. As I said, we're small. And new."

"You activate sleeper cells when needed," said Manny, working it over. "Sounds like Mission Impossible." He was a long admirer of both Ethan Hunt and Tom Cruise, great Americans.

"Close. But that's international espionage."

"What is JFIC?"

"To be blunt, we apprehend high-priority fugitives. Domestic."

Hope stirred in Manny's chest. He was good at his job and he enjoyed it, but he'd reached the phase of life where he wanted more. Not a promotion—he'd take a pay cut to reduce the paper. But more purpose, greater challenge. "I'm in."

She waved it off. "Don't agree yet. I'll provide vague details, give you a few hours to think it over, and then we meet again tonight. I wish I could grant you more time but we're on a clock."

The Director nodded his blocky head.

Manny's gaze bounced with energy between the two. "I'm not good at much in this world. But I can throw men into prison. I'm good at it. I love this country, and protecting it keeps me sane."

"The marshal and sheriff both vouched for you, though they don't know for what." She spread her files across the desk like a fan. "I only work with operatives with an 1811 designation. I can get plenty of those. But not all of them..." She inclined her head. "...wear Armani shirts."

"Brooks Brothers," he corrected her. "Although, if I had to buy an Italian export, it'd be Armani."

"You see? Most men don't care. I work with operatives who do, because not all situations are defused by a gun." She indicated the pistol in his shoulder rig. The revolver. He'd left the Glock in his desk. "The world is changing. Correction—the world has already changed. Footage from cell phones and twenty-four-hour news stations shrink the shadows in which we work best. We're the good guys, but much of what we do is better left outside the courtroom of public opinion. The more we can do quietly, the better."

Manny didn't say so, but he agreed. He thrived in shadows.

She had a crisp straightforward way of speaking. Constant eye contact. "You can imagine how difficult it is to find an operative who..." She slid a file forward, a photograph of Manny clipped to the corner. "...has experience training with SWAT in Los Angles. And..." She slid others across the table. "...worked as a Vice detective in Compton. And earned commendations volunteering to go behind the lines with a Special Forces detail in Central America. And speaks fluent Spanish. And currently works with the local Fugitive Task Force. *And* wears a sports jacket the way you do. Which is a skill unto itself and far more useful than most men realize."

"Plus," said the Director, running a thick finger down his paper. "This impressive arrest record. You apprehended half the East Coast's most wanted list. I spoke with Sergeant Bonham from Los Angeles. He told me about your involvement with the North murders, and that you exposed a corrupt Supervisory Special Agent at the FBI's Los Angeles field office. I remember that damn fiasco."

"I read the classified file. Pretty clever," she said.

Manny dismissed it with a wave of his finger. "She talked in her sleep. Bad habit for a corrupt FBI agent."

The special agent smiled to herself, enjoying Manny's quiet confidence. One of those intangibles which can't be taught.

She said, "If you agree, you'll take a polygraph. And drug test. Tonight."

"Of course."

"You kicked the heroin habit?"

Manny paused. She surprised him—her research had been thorough. He wanted to deny the heroin use. Or at least tell her it hadn't been a habit; it had been a few isolated lapses in judgment in his youth. He wanted to argue with her, demand she admit sometimes the government needed men with baggage. That hard work required hard men and those men didn't come cheap or clean. Insist that, with a childhood like his, some coping mechanisms were to be expected. Tell her she could back down or get the hell out of his office. He let the antagonism swell like a tide, and then recede.

He said, "I'm clean for ten years. Drug test will confirm."

The Director cleared his throat. "Two things in your profile confuse me, Deputy. Why did you turn down the offer to join the Marshal's Special Operations Group last year?"

"I wasn't ready." A half shrug. "Didn't want it to conflict with some other interests. Recently, though, standing in a court room *again*, I regret my decision. What's the other thing?"

"Why do you live with a private investigator? Mackenzie August. Unusual for a man with your salary."

"He's my friend."

"So?"

"He's my only one."

"What about family? We found none."

"Right," said Manny. "That's why I live with August. He's family for me."

"But surely—"

"Where I live doesn't matter, Director."

"Who you live with matters a lot, Deputy."

Manny took a steadying breath. He was being thoroughly vetted; they'd been monitoring his house and checking his finances. They knew he had a fine salary and a fat savings account, and that he volitionally chose to stay at the home of the August family. He didn't begrudge the question—he was aware his living arrangement looked unusual—a house with three men and a toddler. But even though he didn't begrudge the question, he didn't enjoy it either. Largely because he didn't have a great answer.

They weren't asking if he was gay. Even a surface investigation would indicate he wasn't. Did they know he preferred to sleep on the floor? Even more strange, that he preferred to sleep on the floor in Mackenzie's room?

He was unwilling to explain to these federal officials, born into a wealthy country, that he hadn't slept in a room by himself until he was eighteen. He hadn't enjoyed it then and he didn't enjoy it now.

Manny made a subtle motion expressing frustration, a readjustment of his shoulders. He hardly moved but it spoke volumes. The Director leaned backwards in his chair and the Special Agent smiled to herself again. With a trained eye, dangerous men were easy to spot and she possessed such an eye. She had a feeling one of the reasons Martinez lived with his friend was because he hated financial obligations. His credit was so clean it bordered on being suspicious, but that suited her purposes perfectly.

Manny said, "I'm not going into details. Understand? I'll tell you this—I need to live there. I don't use heroin but I need...what's the word? Big fancy word for friendship." He snapped his fingers. "Camaraderie. Right? Living at that house keeps me on the straight path. You looking for a complete human being without flaws, *amigo*? Look elsewhere."

"I have no use for such human beings," she replied. "Pending your blood work and signature, we will formally offer you the assignment. As the Director mentioned, we have a delicate situation and a clock we're running against."

"Give me the details."

The Director cleared his throat again and shook his head. "JFIC is a top secret Special Access Program, hidden within the FBI's intelligence hierarchy. We are unacknowledged and unreported by the FBI, or any other agency. Very few know of its existence for deniability concerns. Once you sign and pass the polygraph, you'll be designated as need-to-know and upgraded to our nation's top security clearance. Until then we tell you very little. Which is for your protection, as well as ours."

She took over. "I'll confide basic operational details, Martinez. No specifics. It begins when our oversight board becomes aware of a target or situation threatening volatility. Our government hates messes. Most messes, they want gone and don't want to know how or why. So I am contacted. I use the considerable resources extended to me by all five agencies aforementioned to do my research and make a decision; is this a job for my department or not? I handle fugitives who are high-profile, high-risk, politically connected, or extremely dangerous—not the kind advertised on the FBI's most wanted list. There is a secondary list, a worse brand of monster. These are fugitives the public is better off remaining ignorant of, and sometimes these targets are best handled without the use of overwhelming force."

"When a scalpel would be better," said the Director. "Rather than a hammer."

Manny asked, "Assassination?"

"No. Not usually," she said. "If I decide the target fits JFIC's criteria, I select one or more of our agents and we get to work. The operation is buried deeply within the veils of secrecy politicians provide to keep their hands clean. Don't ask, don't answer."

"What can you tell me now?"

"The DEA believes a high-profile fugitive is hiding locally. Inside a fortress, for lack of a better word, in the Allegheny Mountains south of Roanoke. The marshal's fugitive task force hasn't been alerted because we'd like it handled quietly. Your assignment would be analysis and apprehension. Or elimination."

Manny nodded. The hairs on his arm stood. "Let's go."

The Special Agent slid a card across. She'd written a number on it. "I insist you think it over. Call me tonight at 9pm. You'll remain a marshal. That's still your job. But when JFIC calls, you answer. Understand?"

Manny picked up the card. He understood.

It was a one-way ticket.

Somehow the card felt hot in his fingertips.

3

An hour later, Manny slid into the leather driving chair of his Chevy Camaro ZL1. Turbocharged, 650 horsepower, six-speed manual transmission—he could've won the Revolutionary War by himself with such a machine. Mosaic black metallic paint. Nothing but the Rat Pack on the radio. Classic American muscle car so powerful he didn't touch the accelerator for three streets.

The radio remained off, his mind full of JFIC and the offer on the table.

He paused at the intersection near Market in the Square. An elderly woman crossed in front of his bumper. She noted the car, peered at the driver, and scowled. Manny reversed and parked illegally. The July air felt hot and thick.

"Let's go." He took the elderly woman by the elbow and steered her in the direction of Scrambled, his favorite breakfast nook. "You and me, we're getting food."

"No quiero comer contigo," she said.

- I don't want to eat with you. -

"Too bad, *amá*. We're eating," Manny replied.

"No molestes a una anciana!"

- Don't bother an old woman! -

Manny guided her under the outdoor tent area to a table. He sat her down. Only one other person was in their section, a businessman, bald. The businessman wrinkled his nose distastefully at the old woman.

In Spanish, she asked, "You are still a cop?"

"A deputy marshal."

She made a motion and a noise like spitting on him. "I hate cops."

"You told me."

A brunette arrived to take their order. Staci. She managed Scrambled and usually let her employees wait the tables but for Manny she couldn't resist.

Manny ordered their famous scrambled eggs for both him and the old woman. The food came, along with orange juice for her and ice water for Manny. Staci waited until Manny pronounced judgment on the eggs—spectacular—then she bounced on her toes and brightly promised to return soon.

The old woman scoffed and in Spanish said, "You're too pretty for your own good."

"Eat," said Manny.

She scowled at her plate but she obeyed. They ate in silence for five minutes, Manny's water glass replenished by Staci each time he took a sip. He picked up the old woman's napkin when she dropped it. Finally, plates clean, the old woman said, "Let me see the photo."

Manny extracted his wallet and withdrew a photograph. He unfolded it twice and slid it across the table, an old polaroid of a young woman laughing. It was creased and fading.

She glared at it and muttered, "You still believe."

"I do. I need her."

"She is dead."

Manny said nothing. A muscle in his jaw flexed.

"Do not bother me about this anymore. Understand? Please. You keep bothering me and I hate it. Give an old woman some money and let her live in peace."

"No, I will not give you money," replied Manny in Spanish. "But I like buying you breakfast."

"Show some respect, cop. Bastard cop.

Manny snatched the photo and waved it, irritably. "This woman? I love her."

"Go look for her in Los Angeles." The old woman rose unsteadily to her feet. Her cheeks were sunken, many of her teeth gone. She stank. "Go back and stay there. Stop being a fool."

4

Ten Years Earlier

MANNY WAS UNDERCOVER, on a personal assignment. So deep undercover that he'd gotten high in the basement of a well-known drug dealer.

It was difficult to suffer years of abuse and emerge clean, and he was still shrugging off demons. Tonight he'd lost the battle, so it seemed.

He'd been out, but for how long? And what the hell was that awful smell?

This wasn't his house. Was it? No, it couldn't be.

He groped for his pistol. Even operating within the depths of delirium, he knew to reach for the gun, but it was gone. He fished blindly.

Or maybe it was his hand that was missing?

A man towered over him, blocking the weak light. "Looking for this? You looking for this, little man?"

Manny needed several seconds to decipher the words. The man blurred and lost focus, like a trick set of reading

glasses. He waved Manny's revolver in his right hand.
With his left, he hit Manny. It was a poorly thrown punch
without conviction. Manny didn't feel it much.

He felt other things, though. His senses thundered.
His eyes ached, ears throbbed, tongue spasmed.

Where *was* he? He couldn't remember...

Oh yes. The heroin den.

Concrete floor. Thin rug. Blue candle in the corner,
upside down, a place for candles. Exposed rafters and
plumbing. A necklace hung on the wall, crucifix pendant.

"This little bitch," said the man above. He had friends.
Looked like maybe two of them. Or...Manny blinked.
Several hundred. "This little bitch, one of Los Angeles'
finest."

From his position on the floor, Manny said, "I'm a
police detective, working for Vice."

It came out, *Mmmtective ww'fice.*

"Oh we know you. Everybody knows Detective
Martinez. The famous Manny, Manny the cop, Manny the
narc." The man laughed. Jewelry flashed at his neck and
ears. "Big detective up in my house smoking beast. Big ass
detective hooked on heroin?"

Manny grinned. "Not hooked."

"*Gee*-sus you a pretty boy. Little pretty bitch, maybe
you quit the five-oh and let me shop you around."

Manny twitched a photograph from his pocket. A
polaroid of a beautiful Hispanic girl, his age, laughing.
"I'm looking for this woman. Have you seen her?"

The man holding his gun didn't reply. Manny sharpened his eyes. The man was black. No...Asian. No...damn,
it was hard to see in this basement.

Manny said, "I heard she was here," or close to it.

The man spoke softly. "You looking for Raquel."

"Her name's Sofia."

"I say her name's Raquel? Her name's Raquel."

"Are you Three Guns?" asked Manny, the words coming out wrong. "This is your heroin den? I heard she was at Three Guns."

The man knocked Manny's hand away, the one with the polaroid. "Bitch, in my basement, you call me—"

Manny hit him. Though Manny had injected heroin not an hour previous, the punch wasn't poorly thrown. Sudden and violent, it lacked no conviction, and he threw with his good hand. Manny had grown up a fighter and he fought still and Three Guns' nose crunched. His upper lip burst against his teeth. The heroin dealer roared.

With the heel of his right boot, Manny kicked the shins out from under Three Guns' friend. Manny swiveled his hips and rose as the friend fell. On his feet, Manny threw a left into the third man's stomach. This man was fat. Manny hit him a right, breaking the fat man's teeth. Even high, Manny dealt violence fluently.

Reality seemed to detach from itself. Music from his childhood blared in his left ear. His vision smeared like an inkblot. He was smiling and he didn't know why.

Oh yes, that's why—heroin.

What a fool he was.

Was that it? Were there any more? He turned in a circle, a disorienting motion near enough to topple him. He hauled Three Guns up. Hefted him by the throat. Three Guns spit on him and swung and missed. Manny head butted him—the man's nasal bones broke, not just cartilage.

"Her name's Sofia," said Manny. "I'm looking for her. She here?"

Three Guns made a groaning noise.

Manny hit him again. And again. His knuckles bruised and bled. He didn't feel it. Three Guns went insensate.

Manny dropped him and looked for someone else to hit. They had Sofia.

An invisible fist drove into his stomach.

An invisible kick almost detached his jaw. He fell. The universe swelled and retracted. Music from his childhood shattered.

Manny's eyes opened. Next to him was the photograph. Drops of blood from his face. He pinched the photograph between his fingers and said to no one, "I'm looking for this woman. Please."

Hands picked Manny up. He did his best to help. He wobbled and swayed. Candles burned in the corner. His assailants were shadow and moonlight silhouettes.

"You a dead detective now," said someone from everywhere and there was laughter.

They were going to kill him. He should care more, probably.

Through the storm of coalescing emotions, euphoria and madness, a newcomer strode into the room. A big man, an angel from heaven, thought Manny.

It was Mackenzie August. His friend. Manny smiled but it hurt. Mackenzie worked homicide. What was he doing here?

Mackenzie August hit the fat man in the head. The fat man fell.

Mackenzie pressed his pistol up another man's nose. "I'm taking Detective Martinez. Any objections?" said August. He said it soft. Death doesn't have to shout.

The man with a gun up his nose whimpered.

With his free hand, Mackenzie flicked the guy's ear. "You got your *ear* tattooed? That's dedication. And I'll make you a deal," he said. "You forget Detective Manny Martinez was here, I won't come back for a month. Deal?"

The man tried to nod but the pistol barrel resisted. Instead he said, "Deal."

Mackenzie nodded at the floor. "Tell Three Guns our deal. He forgets this happened and he gets a month to move his operation. A month of grace, before I return. If he's still here, I kill him."

The world swam as Manny listened to his friend bully the heroin dealers. All of a sudden, he didn't feel so good.

Mackenzie retrieved Manny's revolver and asked him, "Manny, where's your service weapon?"

"Home," said Manny.

"Good. Put away the photograph."

Manny obeyed. Blood dribbled from the corner of his mouth.

"Can you walk?"

Manny tried to respond—nothing came out. Everything was happening so fast and loud. He felt like hot garbage.

Mackenzie picked him up in a fireman's carry. Over his left shoulder. With his right arm, Mackenzie kept his Kimber 1911 ready. He had a long walk out of the house, moving through men who hated cops.

"Good grief, you're fat."

"No'm not," said Manny, hanging upside down. "One-seventy-five, baby. All muscle. I won the belt. But I think I might throw up."

"If you throw up on me, I leave you here to die."

"August?"

"What."

"Thanks," said Manny.

"Shut up. Don't talk. I think you're especially stupid

and I'm angry with you," said August. He went up the stairs, out of the dark basement. Manny watched it happen, looking backwards. The air up here felt warmer.

People were watching. Angry people.

"She's not here, August," he said.

"I know. And you gotta quit looking in these places. You don't possess the fortitude. Did you kill anyone?"

"For'nitude," said Manny, bouncing on August's shoulder. "Stupid word. Thought she'd be here."

Mackenzie August shouted something. At someone Manny couldn't see. That someone shouted back.

August fired his gun at the ceiling. A warning shot.

Manny closed his eyes.

"I promise," he said. No one heard him. It came out, *A'romise.* "I won't ever do this again. I promise."

5

"Manny?"

Staci was on her knees next to his chair. Her hand rested on his thigh, shaking him.

"Manny?"

Manny blinked. Sat up straighter. Gunshot echoes in his ears.

His plate of eggs was empty. The old woman had left. How long was he out? He glanced at his phone—only a few minutes. He had one missed text message, from his roommate, Mackenzie August.

>> You're on dinner tonight. I request some form of charcuterie, preferably hot off the grill.

The hell did charcuterie mean?

"Are you okay?" asked Staci. She shook his leg again. Her eyes were wide and brown. "You're sweating and you look lost."

Manny grinned and wiped his forehead with a napkin. "Sorry. Bad dream."

"You don't look good, Manny. Maybe I should take you

home?" Her hand still rested on his thigh and she squeezed.

"Sounds nice. Maybe so."

"Yes?"

"But," he said, neatly folding and replacing the napkin. "Another day. I'm in no shape to entertain, *mamitá*." Manny stood and dropped forty dollars on the table. For the eggs and for his embarrassment.

Ten minutes later, he motored into an old lot off Centre Avenue NW, a street populated with abandoned warehouses. This part of the city contained corroding junkyards and industrial storage and waste. His Camaro rumbled through the gravel to the back of the lot to a collection of cars at the rusted fence. Two old Nissans and a gleaming black Lexus. He stepped out of the machine and breathed in deeply, savoring the scent of train diesel and coal.

A kid in a red hoodie appeared on the loading dock. Hands in the hoodie pouch, likely holding a pistol.

Manny leaned against his car and called, "Tell Marcus I'm here." The kid, maybe still in his teens, went back in.

From under his Randolph Engineering aviators— made in America; Massachusetts, to be specific—he idly inspected the place. Although the owners intended to give the impression of a forgotten storage yard, Manny saw hints of the truth, of precaution and security. New locks on the doors. Reinforced windows. Hidden security cameras. Small windows in concrete walls to provide firing angles. Fresh gravel for heavy trucks.

Inside the loading dock before him, he knew, there was fifty million worth of cocaine. Maybe another million in firearms.

He could storm the place. Call the marshals and the

sheriff, and make the biggest bust on the East Coast in half a decade. Get his name in the papers, maybe a promotion.

But what fun would that be?

Marcus Morgan emerged to greet him. Tall guy, thin but strong. Black slacks, black shirt, silver buckle and watch. Kept his hair close and wore a thin mustache and soul patch, like Michael Jordan. Deep voice.

He said, "Marshal. Must be important, bringing your unwelcome ass here."

Instead of answering, Manny pressed a button on his key fob and the trunk of the Camaro opened. He reached in and hauled a man out, grunting with the effort. The man wore a red hoodie and his hair was done in short cornrows. He'd been gagged, hands and ankles tied, and he dropped helplessly onto the ground.

"Aw shit," said Marcus Morgan, crossing his arms.

From his boot Manny produced a knife. The man saw the knife and emitted a moan. Manny sliced the binds and the gag, and slid the knife back into his boot. The man on the ground flopped loose like a fish.

Two teenage sentries in the warehouse came to watch.

Marcus Morgan nudged the man on the ground with his loafer. He said, "Morning, Diego. Don't get up yet."

Diego tried to stretch but it hurt. He winced against the sun and rubbed his wrists. "This piece of shit kept me in there all night, Marcus. *All* the damn night. Gimme a gun and I'll kill his family. He don't know me."

Manny, half-sitting on the Camaro, pressed his boot against Diego's face and pushed it into the gravel. From under his arm he produced his heavy revolver.

Marcus Morgan lowered to a crouch by Diego's head. He spoke softly. "Diego. I wouldn't say I'm friends with the marshal. But I ain't his enemy either. Call it mutual respect. And he brings you inside his trunk? Makes me nervous."

"Bitch a got'damn marshal? Let me kill him, Marcus, you let me—"

Manny pressed harder with his boot on Diego's face and the words stopped.

Marcus Morgan scooped a handful of gravel and let them drop one by one. "Why'd the marshal grab you?"

"I don't...I didn't do nothing!" The man's words sounded funny, his cheeks squished together. "I swear to God, Marcus, I don't know what he's doing! He took Milo Wiggins too."

Morgan shifted his gaze. "That true? You took Milo?"

Manny nodded, keeping his eyes on the warehouse. He spun the revolver forward, caught it, then backwards and caught it, like Doc Holliday in that western movie he liked. He still hadn't spoken, which he knew tended to unnerve those he wanted unnerved.

Morgan said, "Damn, marshal. Milo works with the Atlanta guys. Atlanta don't like losing enforcers."

"I told Milo not to come back. *Pendejo* didn't listen. Atlanta guys, they're just like the rest. Only listen to force, not warnings. So I beat the hell out of Milo and took him in."

"And Diego here?"

Manny released his boot from Diego's face and he reached into the Camaro's trunk. He pushed aside the body armor, the ballistic shield and helmet, the baton, and came up with a clear baggie. Inside it, a gray powder. He handed the baggie to Morgan. "Found your boy with heroin."

Morgan squeezed the bridge between his eyes with his

thumb and forefinger. He sighed and held the bag out to Diego. "Where'd you get this?"

"Marcus, this is bull, man. That guy don't—"

"Where'd you get it?"

Diego began to sweat. Nothing good happened when Marcus Morgan spoke quietly. "Jeez-us, Marcus. Okay, damn, whatever. Couple small time guys. Asked me to move a little. Not much, Marcus, I swear."

"We don't touch heroin."

"I mean, I know, man, but—"

"And we oust those who do."

"Oust? Marcus, you know, what the hell? We sell product. Product is product. I don't get it, man."

Marcus Morgan dropped the bag so that it landed on Diego's face. Diego wanted to get up but didn't dare. He'd never been this close to death and he knew it. Morgan pointed with his finger. "See my man, here? See Manny the marshal?"

"Sure, Marcus, I see him."

"Ever wonder why he doesn't get on the radio and bust us? Call in a thousand cops? Wonder why I trust him and he trusts me? See, me and the marshal got a deal. An understanding. We both know that drugs are forever. Can't be stopped. You understand? We live in this fallen world ever since Eve ate that got'damn apple, right? People break bad, it's gonna happen. If I close up shop and leave, what'll happen next? Someone else show up soon. Guaranteed. Someone worse. Nature hates a vacuum, Diego. You know what that means?"

"Sure, Marcus, I know what that means. Nature hates a vacuum."

Manny, leaning against his car, smiled. He kept

thumbing back the hammer on his revolver and carefully releasing it. Diego flinched at each click.

"I know what it means too, Diego," said Marcus Morgan. "So does the marshal. He knows if I go then someone else shows up. Someone worse. Cause I hate violence and I hate heroin. So me and the marshal, we cut a deal. I keep my shit buttoned up, I keep heroin and meth and crack off the street, me and him got no trouble. You follow?"

"Yeah, I follow. Marcus, I swear, man I didn't—"

"You didn't what? You didn't follow orders, that's what." Marcus picked up the bag again. Pinched the edges and tugged it open, then upended the bag. The gray powder, thousands worth, dumped onto Diego's face. He coughed and rubbed at his eyes. Marcus stood with the grunt all men his age make. He dusted his hands and asked, "Milo running heroin too?"

Manny said, "Didn't find any. He had a couple girls I let go."

"Appreciate you not acing Diego or taking him downtown."

Diego stood with damaged pride, his cramped muscles relenting slowly. "I don't get it, man. Cocaine, heroin, what's the got'damn difference?"

"Way I see it, *amigo,*" said Manny. "We can't stop it all. Some stuff's gonna get in. But crack and meth and heroin, those destroy cities. Those kill people slow, rotting the city from the inside. I like it here. Roanoke's a good city. So we let in the coke, keep out the rest. It's the best I can do."

"We could make a lot more scratch," said Diego. "Other cities doing it."

Manny kept spinning the gun, catching sunlight each rotation. "Then move there. I don't like you anyway."

"Put the gun away. Can't shoot me. You a cop."

Manny grabbed the handle, halting the spin. The barrel pointed at Diego. "Bang." He spun it again. "Might be surprised. Cops shoot people. Besides, I'm not a good one."

"So you on the take?"

He caught the grip again and said, "Pow." Spun it some more around his pointer finger. "On the take? No. Keep this in mind. The best police, like me, don't play by rules. Write that down."

"Best police." Diego snorted. "Big time lawman."

"Lawman in pursuit of life and liberty and girls. Like a true American."

"You a true damn spic, what you are."

Marcus Morgan shook his head. He took a step back, away from the marshal. Diego's fate was out of his hands now.

Manny said, "I'm a damn spic who loves this country. And hates guys who make it worse."

"You love this country," repeated Diego with a laugh. "This country's a shit hole, ask me."

Manny's revolver flashed as he snatched the grip again. He fanned his left thumb, pointer finger, and middle finger across the hammer in one smooth motion. Each finger grabbed the hammer, tugged it back, and dropped it. Three fingers, three gunshots, so quick it sounded like an automatic burst. He practiced it at the range weekly, like an old west gunslinger.

The first bullet hit Diego in the stomach. The second in the chest. The third in the forehead. He staggered backwards and fell, screaming.

One, two, three rounds fired, counted Manny. And three remaining in the cylinder. He always counted.

Marcus growled, "Marshal, what the hell? Neighbors call the cops."

Manny spun the gun and holstered it. "I'm the cops. And I don't like disparaging comments about my country."

Diego kept screaming, rolling across the gravel.

The two guys at the warehouse waited on Marcus to tell them what to do. Shoot the marshal! Run!

"I say that right? Disparaging?" asked Manny.

"Sounds like a word August taught you."

"Hey," said Manny, loud enough to get Diego's attention. "Ay! You notice you ain't dead, *pana*?"

Diego's noises changed to groans and he pawed at his forehead.

Marcus smiled. "How the hell he's still alive?"

"Shot him with wax bullets. I told you, some guys need force, not warnings. Don't talk bad about my country."

"Wax bullets? That a thing?"

"Make'em myself. They hurt but he'll live. When I carry the Glock, I keep wax in the revolver." He jerked his head to the side and led Marcus down the gravel lot, twenty yards away from prying ears. "I got a weird question for you."

"Aight," said Marcus Morgan.

"I heard about a fortress in the hills, south of here. In the mountains. Good hiding place for well-connected fugitives. You know it?"

"Fortress in the mountains. Yeah, I know the place. It's big league."

Manny took off his aviators and nodded to himself. Cleaned the lenses on his jacket. "Hard to get in?"

Marcus chuckled. "Impossible, without a got'damn army. Know what's good for you, you won't try."

"Who's there now?"

"Got no idea. I've only been once. The District Kings don't handle the property. We just rent it now and then."

"From who?"

Marcus shrugged. "One of those underworld groups providing resources to rich gangsters. You know, in the grand scheme of things, Marshal, me and you pretty small fish. The guys who rent that place? They ain't small fish. Follow?"

Manny followed.

A big fish, in an underworld fortress in the mountains. A fish that needed to be caught.

His day kept getting better.

6

That night, Manny sat on his front porch digesting a half-pound burger and kale salad. With him on the porch sat the three other men living at the house—well, two men and a toddler.

Manny lounged in a rocking chair. Mackenzie's son, the toddler, Kix, leaned into the crook at his elbow, asleep.

Two years ago, Manny had arrived in Roanoke a broken man and Mackenzie August took him in. An uncommon friendship sprung from the bond men in the line of duty share. Manny had shaken off the PTSD long enough to hold down the deputy marshal job and had lived here ever since. They lived on a corner lot in the Grandin neighborhood of Roanoke, Virginia. One of those established neighborhoods with hundred-year-old pine and maple, and a ribbon of sidewalk laid across the front lawn. Their house was a restored 1925 vintage foursquare with a wraparound porch. Manny didn't care exactly what that meant but it was nicer than his old apartment in Los Angeles.

Citronella candles crackled, glazing the scene with a

cheery glow, and keeping the mosquitos at bay. Mackenzie August and his father Timothy, a local elementary school principal, sat in rocking chairs on either side of a chess board, glaring at the battlefield.

Mackenzie August looked, Manny thought, like the guy who played Mad Max. Where Manny was light and quick, August was thick and powerful and taller by two inches at least. They boxed regularly at the gym, but only as training partners. Who'd win a real fight? They'd probably kill each other. He was a well respected private detective in town.

The porch's fan kept up a steady stream of air.

Ice tinkled in Manny's glass as he took a sip of his margarita and lowered it. "Are you satisfied with your charcoal hootery?"

Mackenzie August asked, "Are you trying to say charcuterie?"

"That *is* what I said."

"Burgers were elite, Manny, thank you," said Timothy, the eldest of the men. His chin rested on his fist. He released a resigned sigh and moved his pawn, and returned to his glass of scotch.

Mackenzie hmm'ed over the move. "Agreed, Manny. You are the Rachael Ray of your ilk."

"Rachael Ray, the chubby white lady who cooks?"

"She's not chubby."

"Some wind sprints wouldn't hurt, though," said Manny. Kix adjusted himself on Manny's lap and sighed in his sleep.

Timothy August drained his glass, and he said, "Something's bothering you, Manny."

"Nothing *bothers* me, señor. I am merely a Latino deep in thought."

"What about?"

"A job opportunity. Kinda," said Manny.

Mackenzie raised up from his thoughtful scrutiny of the chessboard. "An entirely new profession?"

"More like new responsibilities, in the same position."

"The Marshal's Special Operations Group?"

"No, it's a domestic black ops team. The supervisor is a woman named Weaver who works for the FBI, I'd still be a marshal, but when she calls, I go."

"You're not allowed to talk about it, I bet," said Mackenzie, and he sipped his margarita.

"Sí."

"But you're going to anyway."

"Of course."

"What does the black ops team do?" asked Mackenzie.

"Chase *desperados*. The kind requiring precision instead of, ah, overwhelming force. The kind of guy who doesn't make the top ten lists because politicians don't wanna know."

"*Very* black ops."

"I think so."

"You die, not many people know why," said Mackenzie.

"Right."

"You'd be good at it."

Manny nodded. "Obviously."

"Go for it. Because I am a professionally trained inspector, I was able to detect you getting a little antsy."

Manny frowned. "I do not get antsy."

"You're bored. The routine's got you down. Too many prisoner transports. You like the structure the gig provides, along with intermittent autonomy, but now you're antsy. You need more. You're an American gentleman, but also you're an action junkie. You're not a meek man. You weren't dealt meek cards. Sometimes, you gotta let the freak flag fly."

"You had me until the end. Freak flag. One of those weird things white people say."

Mackenzie moved his knight, a dashing and triumphant move in his eyes. "Only us elite honkies."

Kix made another sighing noise and shifted on Manny's arm.

Timothy August asked, "Do you want to do this, Manny? Are you dissatisfied with your current position?"

Manny leaned back on his rocking chair and hoisted Kix so he slept on his chest, using his shoulder as a pillow. Manny patted the toddler's back absently. "I am not well educated like you, señor August. Nor intuitive and patient like Mack. I can't do what you do. What I do well is conflict. This would be a greater challenge. And maybe I'm antsy."

Timothy finished his scotch, stood, and went inside. Through the open window they heard the sound of a single ice cube dropping into his glass, then a splash of liquor. He returned and swirled it.

"I'm a little out of my league. You two men have a code, don't you. Some reason to continue the work you do, which requires violence. You both chose vocations which are hard and threaten your life. It's a code soft men like me can never understand."

Manny shrugged. "Don't overthink it, *señor*. I don't have much in this world. Don't need much. But what I have? I have this family and I have my country. And if my country asks me to bleed, I do."

Timothy asked, "It's that simple? I mean no offense

but sometimes I look at our country and I think, what the hell is going on? Is it worth bleeding for?"

"It is. If I have a code, it's a simple one. I do what I think makes America better."

"That's highly subjective."

"Use smaller words. Don't forget, I was born a humble Argentinian."

"I thought it was Puerto Rican?" said Timothy.

"It's both. The hell does subjective mean?"

Mackenzie grinned at Manny's many layers. "He means, what makes America better isn't black and white. It's a gray area."

"I thrive in gray areas," said Manny. "But for me, it's a black and white issue."

"Which political party do you align with?" asked Timothy.

"You know the guy in the White House right now? I like him. You know the guy in the White House a few years ago? I liked him too. The guy who wins it next? Or girl? I already like that person. Black and white."

Timothy scratched at his jaw. A well-educated and erudite man, a constant consumer of non-fiction literature, a man making his living in academia, who prided himself on his political positions, found himself befuddled and humbled by the blind patriotism. Somehow the shallow loyalty struck him as deeply profound.

Timothy leaned forward and pushed over his king. "I surrender. My situation is hopeless."

"Pick up your king, old man," said Mackenzie. "A resilient and resourceful opponent could still squirm free."

Timothy stood. "I'm going to bed."

"Coward."

"Maybe you should treat your father with more respect."

"Maybe you should read a book on chess theory before you fall asleep," said Mackenzie.

"Good night, American gentlemen."

He went inside and Mackenzie and Manny listened to the buzzing of cicadas a few minutes.

"When do you start?"

"Tomorrow," said Manny. "They got a situation."

Mackenzie stood and took his son out of Manny's arms. Kix sighed but didn't wake. "You're accepting the assignment?"

"You didn't talk me out of it."

"I wouldn't. You're the most dangerous man I've ever met."

"Obviously," said Manny.

"It speaks well of this black ops group that they recognize it."

"Sí."

"I got your back, if you need it," said Mackenzie.

"I know."

Left alone on the front porch, Manny didn't hesitate. He finished his margarita and eyed the slip of paper with Weaver's telephone number. He dialed the number and a woman's voice answered.

"Yes?"

"I want in. Let's do this."

"Good. You see the car?" As the woman spoke, an electric car hummed quietly into view and stopped in front of their house. "That's your ride."

Manny whistled. "Spooky trick."

The line disconnected.

The car was a Tesla. As he approached, the rear door

unlocked. He shifted his weight slightly, testing the reassuring weight of the gun on his belt, opened the door, and slid in. The car ghosted forward without a sound. There was no driver.

"*Ay dios mio,*" said Manny. "Spooky as hell."

A voice came over the speakers. "Relax, Deputy Martinez. It's a short trip. See you in five minutes."

7

The Tesla turned onto a dark street downtown. Kirk Avenue was laid with charming brick, the sidewalks lined with young hedge maples. At a nondescript door the car stopped. The FBI's Roanoke office. Manny's door unlocked and he got out.

The stern green-eyed woman from earlier met him and shook his hand again, a touch more firmly now. She said, "You're sure?"

"I'm in."

"My name is Weaver. SSA in the FBI's Criminal Investigation Division, Violent Crimes Unit. Follow me." She led him through the dark office, satisfying two points of biometric security measures. In the back, they found buzz cut waiting.

He said, "Deputy, glad to have you. Name's Douglas, Director of Special Operations for the DEA." He slid a neat stack of papers Manny's way. "Sign these and we'll proceed."

Manny held up a hand. "I have a stipulation. Shouldn't cause any trouble. I get a codename?"

Special Agent Weaver nodded. "Yes, as do the others. In my files you'll be known as—"

"Sinatra."

Her eyebrow rose slightly. "You're kidding."

"My stipulation. I want to be Sinatra."

Douglas's face turned downward with displeasure. "Good hell, Martinez, this is national security, not a joke. The time we spent—"

"I make no joke, Director Douglas. And no disrespect. I want my codename to be Sinatra." Manny crossed his arms.

"As in, Frank Sinatra?"

"My opinion, he's one of the great Americans of the twentieth century. Hardworking, stylish, and tough. I love his music, plus white people relax around a guy named Sinatra rather than Martinez. A pilot gets to pick his call-sign and I get to pick my codename. I choose Sinatra."

Douglas shared a glance with Weaver, a look conveying frustration and fear they'd wasted their time with a juvenile deputy marshal playing games. If they couldn't trust his judgment now, granting him autonomy in the field was impossible. But Weaver nodded, confident in her selection; Manny was a man who took America more seriously than most. He was dedicated and punctilious and thorough and absolutely lethal, and at the moment he wasn't being boyish—he was being Manny.

"I see no issue with that," she said.

"Good."

A third individual came in. Bland looking guy, small features. He pierced a vein in Manny's arm and filled vials with blood. He connected Manny to a machine and asked questions for thirty minutes. Some deeply personal and

Manny fought to keep anger out of his voice. Douglas and Weaver watched silently, half an eye on him and half an eye on the monitor. Finally the man nodded, disconnected Manny, and left.

Manny signed his name to a dozen weighty nondisclosure agreements. Weaver said, "Welcome aboard, Sinatra."

Manny winked. "Sounds good, right?"

"Tell me, Deputy," said Douglas, sliding photographs and newspaper clippings across the desk. Manny recognized them immediately: the national wildlife refugee standoff, spearheaded by Ammon Bundy; the disaster at Waco; the Ruby Ridge siege; the botched arrest of mobster Buster Wertz, and the collateral damage of eight civilian deaths. "What do these have in common?"

"Embarrassment for the American government."

"Correct. These are situations when perhaps one or two highly skilled operational agents could have mitigated disaster. When a scalpel, instead of the hammer, could have saved time and resources and lives and, yes, embarrassment."

"It's getting worse every year," said Weaver. "With cell phone documentation. We can't blow our nose without outrage online. Thus, the extreme importance of JFIC."

Manny scanned the various other photos. "Not all these involve drugs, Director. But you're with the DEA."

"The reason I accompanied Special Agent Weaver today is that our current situation does."

Weaver slid him another collection of photographs, of an impressive mountain chateau, taken from above. Struck Manny as a modern day castle. Extremely isolated. Surrounding walls, a courtyard at the middle, four large superstructures connected by covered walkways...he looked closer and found a second and thicker security wall circumventing the campus through the trees. She said, "This is the aforementioned fortress. Built near Pine Mountain in Kentucky, near the Virginia border."

"Not many people in that part of the state," mused Manny. "Three hours from here?"

"Four," she replied. "We nicknamed it the Appalachian Palace. Built in the late 1960s by gangsters from New Jersey, and then sold in the 80s to a shadowy umbrella group loosely connected with various organized crime syndicates around the globe. A completely self-sufficient and almost entirely impregnable compound. If we wanted to force our way in, we'd need military-grade munitions. There is at least one bunker going fifty feet into the mountain, and potentially many others so even if we had legal reason to invade, and even if we brought enough firepower to knock down the doors, those inside could slip out the back easily and then we'd be chasing them all over the East Coast. And avoiding that scenario is precisely the reason for JFIC's existence."

Douglas rumbled, "We know for a fact Whitey Bulger stayed there in the 90s, and we suspect El Chapo took up residence in 2010 for nearly six months, though we only discovered it after the fact. Other guests include Meyer Lansky and Fuentes, plus lesser-known but more powerful overseas criminals."

Manny nodded, his hackles rising. He felt like a hound held on a leash, ready to pounce. "Who is the shadowy umbrella group who owns the Palace?"

"We don't know," said Weaver, vexation imparted between her syllables. "I refer to them as APOG, for Appalachian Palace Ownership Group. Organized crime syndicates get more and more sophisticated the higher up the ladder they go. This ownership group does everything legal, even pays their property taxes ahead of time. Their money gets lost quickly in overseas accounts, making it hard to trace. We have no legal reason to get a warrant. From what we can tell, residents pay ten grand a night."

Manny whistled. "I'm in the wrong line of work."

"Eleven days ago, Data Intercept started getting tower pings from the Palace. Sudden increased cellphone usage. PRISM captured fragments of encrypted phone calls and texts; we decoded enough to conclude an international terrorist has moved in."

"Who is he?"

"She," said Douglas, handing him yet another file. "Calls herself El Gato or sometimes Gato Rico. We don't know her true identity but we know she's a broker between various governments in Central America and drug cartels. The DEA attempted an arrest four years ago and failed. Spectacularly. Local news picked it up but thankfully the national networks didn't. Else I'd be out of a job."

There was very little information. Manny stared at the words El Gato and Honduras and deep within his subconscious chimes began to ring. Old memories he couldn't immediately place.

"The Cat," he muttered.

"Yes." She watched his reaction. "She fled after the DEA came close but it appears she recently returned. We want to know why, and preferably ask her that question inside a holding cell."

"That fortress is heavily fortified, with both a permanent security staff and El Gato's private detail," said

Douglas. "She travels with an armed guard of ten men, based on our previous experience."

"Good thing I'm expendable," said Manny. "Why me? Why not one of your other sleeper agents? Because I speak Spanish?"

"There are two reasons why I decided to approach you, Sinatra," she said, trying out his codename. All parties in the room at once decided it fit and bore no further comment. Her fingers drummed absently on the final manila folder, one she hadn't given him yet. "The first reason is the clock I mentioned. We don't have much time. APOG reserved a private jet through one of its subsidiary financial companies, scheduled to depart Saturday morning from Roanoke's airport. Five days from now. APOG doesn't know we're aware of the subsidiary. Our best guess is, she plans to fly out on that jet. But that's merely a guess. Because we aren't positive El Gato is truly at the Palace, because we don't know conclusively who the private jet is reserved for, and because of the previous disaster when we tried to arrest her, we don't want to attempt capture at the public airport. Her involvement with cartels and foreign governments makes this extremely sensitive. We need another plan. That's why you're being activated."

"That flight could be a decoy," said Manny.

"Certainly. But for what?"

"What is the second reason you choose me?" he asked, though he'd already guessed the reason. And it was a doozy.

Weaver slid a large glossy photograph free from her manila folder and handed it to him. A beautiful Hispanic brunette smiling at a cocktail party. "This is El Gato. Our only confirmed photograph."

Manny nodded, his lips pressing together.

"The second reason I choose you is simple. El Gato contacted the DEA and invited you to dinner tomorrow evening."

8

Manny paced the FBI's conference room, hands on his hips. He cut an angry and striking figure—Special Agent Weaver was forced to remind herself she was his superior officer, and he was her operational field agent; she was not a woman and he was not a man, a reality usually not difficult to maintain. Then again, not many men were made like Manny Martinez.

Sinatra, that is.

She said, "As soon as we received the request, we suspected you two have a history."

"I knew El Gato," said Manny, a muscle in his jaw flexing. "In Los Angeles. She was small time then, or so I thought. Her real name's Catalina García."

Weaver punched that detail into her phone. He'd blurted out a fact they'd unsuccessfully spent hundreds of hours researching.

"Romantic?" asked Douglas.

"Obviously. Look at her."

"Normally this would disqualify you from the assignment," said Weaver. "But under these special circumstances, your relationship is our biggest lead."

"What does she want with you?"

Manny waved away the question. "I don't know. We didn't part on good terms. And we haven't communicated for a decade."

"You still want the assignment," said Weaver. It wasn't a question.

"*Sí.* I always thought Catalina needed a good spanking, set her straight."

Douglas's eyes narrowed. "Good hell, Deputy, this day and age, your choice of vocabulary—"

"*Venga!*" snapped Manny. "You know what I meant. Maybe we don't bicker over word choice, Director, when more serious matters press."

Douglas turned a faint shade of purple.

"She's quite attractive," said Weaver.

Manny paused by the photograph. "Looks like she had her nose done since I saw her. Old one looked fine. I told her so."

"Here's how this will work, Sinatra. Director Douglas leaves on a flight tonight. He was never here. I leave tomorrow. I'm working on eight projects at the moment, but I will coordinate with local law enforcement if absolutely necessary. However, my sleeper agents don't work entirely alone. You need support in the field and we've already cleared Noelle Beck. She'll be your technician."

That stopped Manny. "Noelle Beck? The cute computer geek in my office? Isn't she a Mormon?"

"That's irrelevant. She's not there by accident. She was already on loan to the Marshal's office from the NSA, cyber division, so I transferred her to Roanoke. She assisted one of my agents a year ago and she already has top secret clearance."

"Does Beck even carry a gun?"

"She graduated from Georgetown and went into the Air Force, then the NSA. She's a brilliant analyst and technician. At my request, Marshal Warren will deputize her or you can do it yourself. She had military training in the Air Force and she's perfect for your assignment. You'll both be granted a Supremacy License, a government wide discretionary permit pursuant to the national security clause."

Manny didn't know such a license existed and he said so.

Weaver replied, "A little known subsection in the 2012 National Defense Authorization Act. The licenses were proactively issued by the President himself, and the FBI's authorization to distribute them remains in place until the law changes. It's a posse comitatus workaround. The current man in office, I imagine, doesn't know the Supremacy Licenses exist."

Douglas stood and handed Manny an iPad. "This device erases itself in five days and has no ability to transfer data. Everything we know about El Gato and the Appalachian Fortress is on here. You have five days before that plane leaves. Five days to prevent a costly embarrassment for the American government. We need answers. Is she really there? Why did she return to American soil? What are her plans? And how can we arrest her without a costly and violent showdown?"

"I'll read it tonight," said Manny, accepting the iPad. "Brief Beck in the morning. Attend the dinner tomorrow evening at the Palace, give Catalina a good spanking, and deliver her to you trussed up like a pig."

"Good hell," said Douglas again, rubbing at his eyes.

9

Ten Years Earlier

MANNY MARTINEZ STOOD on the tarmac at the Los Angeles International Airport, the whistling wind searing his scalp, which he kept shaved. Hands in his pockets, chin set stubbornly.

A small queue of passengers formed a line, boarding a turboprop Dash-8, a small airliner bound for Honduras. So small the airport didn't bother with a jetway. A brunette woman, about his age with fiery brown eyes, squeezed his arm.

In Spanish, he said, "Don't get on that plane, Catalina."

"Don't let me go alone, Manuel. I am out of words to plead with you."

"You are flying to a land of lies. Trust me. I tried it."

The woman's brothers waited near the small plane, bags slung around their shoulders, arms crossed. She shouted over the swirling airport noises, "Not lies. A land of gold."

"Gold? Everyone there is poor."

"Not if you know the right people."

"And you do?"

She nodded. "I *am* the right people. Come with me. You'll be rich."

Finally he turned his eyes onto her. Hurt, angry eyes. "I'm a cop. You go to join a cartel."

"Not a cartel, a revolution."

"A coup," he snapped.

"If necessary. Don't call yourself a cop, Manuel. You are more than that."

"That's the thing, Catalina. I'm not. And it's all I can do, right now."

They made a dramatic scene, the beautiful woman tugging at her handsome lover. Nearby passengers had no choice but to stare. Her brothers glared murderously at them.

With her free hand, she wiped her eyes. "When you grew up in those lands, you were nothing. Fate brought us together. You'll return as a king, now."

"King of the nothings."

"If it helps, think of it as business."

"Another lie."

She struck him in the face. Openhanded. He winced and bore it, the way he'd learned growing up. "I waited my entire life to tell a man I love him. And he betrays me."

"I'm not the one leaving."

"I *have* to."

"You choose to. Remain here and I'll take care of you."

She made a scoffing sound. "On your salary."

"It's enough."

"It's nothing."

"Not to me. To me, it's everything."

She snaked a hand inside his jacket and jerked out a polaroid of a beautiful woman smiling. "This photo, always this photo. You stay for her. But she abandoned you. The same way you abandon me."

"It's not just for her, Catalina. If I return, it'll be the end. Of me."

"The only reasons my brothers haven't killed you is because of me, you know that."

"It'll take all of them."

Despite the anger, she smiled. "You're right, you know. It would. You are special, Manuel. You know it. I know it. We need you."

"I can't go."

"I can't *stay*. And you need me, *pendejo*. When I'm gone, you'll have nothing. You'll be nothing."

He didn't respond immediately. Her words clanged against the truth, loud, causing internal reverberations. He shook off the sense of falling and said, "My job. That's what I'll have."

"Pathetic."

"I know. But it's enough."

"For how long?"

He shrugged. "I don't know. Long as I can."

The pitch of the airplane's engine changed and the ground service guys called for her. Time to go.

She said, "You'll never see me again."

"I believe you. Because if you go, they'll kill you."

"Not if we kill them first."

"That life is nothing but pain. *Trust* me."

Catalina was close. Manny read it—the indecision and fear in her face. She did trust him. She didn't want to get on that plane. No one prefers Honduras over Los Angeles, he thought. And she loved him. She was close...but she needed him to beg. Needed to be needed. She needed him to swear fealty and plead and promise...she needed the one thing Manny couldn't give. Groveling felt tantamount to quitting, to surrender. Might as well ask him to fly. He'd begged as a kid and got nothing.

Manny Martinez would never need anyone ever again. He'd asked her to stay and she said no. Any woman who wanted to be begged? To hell with her. He felt his face harden, especially around the eyes.

She saw it.

She threw the polaroid down in disgust. He pinned it with the toe of his boot before the tarmac vicissitudes plucked it away. "So long. Cop. Good luck finding her. Or yourself."

"Go," said Manny with a jerk of his chin. He let the anger swell like armor to keep the pain at bay. "Your brothers wait. Enjoy your short life. Maybe they'll bury you with your money."

"What will they bury you with, Manny? Nothing but that photo. You don't even know who you are. You will regret this, Manuel Martinez."

He already did. He already regretted everything.

Only after she boarded the plane did he allow his heart to shatter.

10

Manny woke on the floor. He lay still a few minutes, thoughts cloudy with El Gato. He rose then, rolled and tied off his flat air mattress, and slid it under the boxspring. Mackenzie turned over, under the covers and still asleep. Manny's insides twisted with a familiar sensation—not embarrassment, exactly, about sleeping on Mackenzie's floor. More like vague guilt. Ideally he should be beyond this fear. He picked his heavy .357 revolver off the floor, shoved his pillow next to the rolled air mattress, and left the room.

In the bathroom he showered and stretched his back loose, and softly stamped his right foot to restore sensation, a residual effect from an old knife wound. He dried his hair and moved into his own bedroom. The atmosphere held a hint of cologne and gun oil. He dropped the towel and examined himself in the mirror, a weekly ritual. He was tall, slightly over six feet, lean and well muscled, drawing comparisons to Cristiano Ronaldo, the international soccer star with thick black hair. His torso was crisscrossed with scars from a misspent youth and his arms decorated with tattoos from his arrogant twenties. He didn't have love handles but he eyed the area anyway with displeasure—burning fat proved harder the closer he got to forty.

His closet and two wardrobes were kept in pristine condition—nothing but crisp corners and pressed fabric and jewelry. His outfit? Made in America. He dressed in 5.11 khakis made in California; a slim-fitting button-down Brooks Brothers shirt from North Carolina; skinny black tie and beige sports coat out of New Orleans; a blue-faced luxury watch manufactured in Lancaster; and leather Keen boots from Portland. He holstered the two firearms —a required service pistol, the compact Glock 27, on his belt, and his preferred Smith & Wesson revolver in the shoulder rig. He shot himself in the mirror with his thumb and forefinger.

So American he might as well be Clint Eastwood.

Or maybe John Wick, the better dresser.

He descended into the darkness of the main level and switched on the light. The interior was Craftsman with the walls removed, creating an entirely open space. The marble counters gleamed from polishing, as did the hardwood floors. From the kitchen he used a remote to power on the television in the living room and he thumbed down the volume.

He brewed a pot of strong coffee—beans from Columbia. America had few deficiencies, in his opinion. But one of them? The inability to grow competent coffee beans.

He poured the coffee into a Yeti Rambler mug. Into the Rambler he mixed heavy cream and cartilage and organic butter, and he frothed it until the coffee was thick and rich. Not an extra carbohydrate to be found.

He sipped and switched between CNN, Fox News, and MSNBC. Real Americans got their news from multiple sources and divined the truth, in his opinion. Diverse viewpoints were good. Only a fool let someone else tell him what to believe.

Catalina, he thought. How could the DEA be after little Catalina?

Mackenzie arrived a few minutes later, yawning.

August said, "You think maybe you're the only federal marshal who sleeps on the floor every night?"

"Only one tough enough to."

"Maybe tough isn't the right word. Perhaps fatuous and puerile."

"Those are fake words. How sad for you. Words you're searching for are plucky and Machiavellian," said Manny, bluffing August wouldn't force him to define either. He had a dim awareness toward the definition of plucky.

August paused at the refrigerator. "You're Machiavellian?"

"Obviously." Manny indicated his mug. "I'll make you coffee."

"You make me a cup of your witches brew and I'll shoot it."

"This witches brew is fit for Abraham Lincoln, amigo. It's a super food. All the nutrients you need."

"I like my coffee the way Thomas Jefferson liked it," said August. "Black."

Manny shot him a piercing and suspicious glance, inspecting for slight to the forefathers. But he saw no malice. "Just don't eat oatmeal."

"Maybe you shut up, Abraham. Maybe I'll eat two bowls of oatmeal and pour a third into your pillow case."

Manny pulled the Brooks Brothers shirt loose from his

pants to expose his abdominals. His torso was ridged with muscle and the crevices sharpened as he flexed. "Look at this, Mack. See the muscles? Abs are made in the kitchen. And not with oatmeal."

"Abs are made in the kitchen?"

"Of course."

August nodded with his chin. "You shave your chest and stomach?"

Manny frowned. "No."

"Yeah you do. Thinking about joining a boy band, Abraham?"

"I don't and even if I do, who cares. You're only jealous, *pendejo*."

Mackenzie went back upstairs with his coffee. Soon after, Timothy August left for the day.

Manny sat in the reading chair and skimmed his JFIC assignment on the iPad. He knew it all. And yet still couldn't believe it.

Noelle Beck parked in front of his house an hour later. He came out on the lawn, choosing not to comment on her Honda Accord, the base LX sedan, which was under-powered.

Manny maintained strict rules about office coed fraternization and he'd forced himself to see Beck merely as someone to annoy. She was tall and trim, like she ran cross country. Her face bordered on being too thin but it gave her good cheekbones and an excellent jawline. She always kept her brown hair in a bun and her shirt buttoned to the top. He'd never seen her without the same fitted blue blazer.

She looked pretty, Manny decided, as she got out of the car, even if he preferred she ran track instead of cross country. Short distances produced rounder muscles. Fury over stamina.

"*Buenas dias,* Beck."

She smiled and Manny was charmed. "I'm new to town and know very few people. It's about time you invited me over."

"Don't get your hopes up. We're not allowed."

"I'm a Latter-day Saint. I strictly see you as a terrifying masculine threat in danger of eternal damnation, But I like your house. They must pay you more."

"They should. Do you even carry a gun?"

"As of thirty minutes ago, I am deputized. I was given a service piece. Do you even know how to debug lines of Java?"

"Shut up, Beck. Don't bring that computer jargon to mi casa. My housemates and I share the mortgage. Also, sorry for saying shut up."

She stopped and indicated the lawn. "Wow, look at your flower beds. Clean lines. Trim shrubs. No weeds. You're quite the gardener."

"I do not garden. Come inside."

Beck followed him in, ignoring years of careful religious grooming that taught her this situation was fraught with peril. Alone in a man's house! She grinned to herself, enjoying the scandal. She just wouldn't look at him, that's all. His jacket was off, his sleeves rolled up. She wondered if he had the shirts tailored, because they fit his broad shoulders and trim waist so well...

...she just wouldn't look closely at him, that's all, she told herself again.

"Manny." She stopped in the television room. From her position she could see the entire level, including the cozy reading nook, the television room, the gleaming kitchen, the back deck, and both staircases. Hands on her hips. "Your house is..."

"Yes?"

"Breathtaking. Do you have a cleaning service?"

"No. We are grown-ass men. We clean up after ourselves."

"Did you hire an interior decorator?"

"Of course not."

"Manny, be serious." She pointed at the oriental rug, the built-in shelves, the floor in the kitchen. "Someone vacuumed recently. The corners are clean. This wooden sculpture thingy has no dust. Your marble counters shine. Your books are exact. This looks like a model home."

"You live in a pig sty?"

She gestured at the coffee table. "Even the television remotes are lined up. And..." She paused to take a deep breath. "This place smells like...cologne and leather."

"The men who live here, we are fast idiots."

"You mean fastidious."

"That's what I said. Do you want coffee?"

She ran her hand along the couch. "Why's the leather so soft?"

"I rub in conditioner."

"That's a real thing?" she said. "Did you do this for me?"

Manny made a snorting noise. "Get ahold of yourself, Beck."

Mackenzie August came down the stairs, carrying his son Kix. He nodded at Manny and Beck and said, "Don't mind me and the boy. We're late and leaving. Kix can't seem to shake his hangover."

Manny made truncated introductions.

"You both live here?" asked Beck, impressed with Mackenzie's bulk and height.

"I told you I had housemates. White girls never listen?"

"Back later tonight," said Mackenzie, going through the screen door. "Good luck saving the planet from malfeasants." He was gone.

Beck lowered onto a kitchen stool at the counter. What a fascinating home. Can I come over more often!"

"No. Did you get made fun of in high school?"

"A little."

"Let me guess. You thought you were too tall. And you graduated valedictorian. You were good with computers and you felt awkward about everything you did. At Georgetown you didn't date because the boys had no morals. In the Air Force the men were beneath you. And the Mormon thing makes things tricky. Now you're married to career advancement. How close am I?"

"I dated *some*."

"You're hot now, Beck. You're not too tall, you're just right. You're a kick-ass NSA analyst, not a nerd in high school. Which means you don't ask people if you can come over more often. You do what you want."

"You just said I couldn't come over."

"I objected to you asking, like you're a loser. Are you a loser, Beck?"

"I don't think so."

"You're not but you're a mess. You gotta figure this out on your own time." He held up the iPad and waved it. "I joined JFIC. Our assignment begins immediately. Read these files and get up to speed."

She accepted the device, choosing not to dwell on his bizarre, backward compliments.

He said, "I have a meeting tonight, four hours south-west of here. You're my assistant."

"Technician, you mean." She powered on the iPad. "Call me your assistant once more and I'll give your personal computer a virus."

"I don't have a personal computer."

"That can't be true."

"I spend my money on gin and clothes, not video games" He tapped the iPad. "Read."

"Give me the short version, before I do."

"International crime broker named El Gato is holed up in a fortress nearby. DEA doesn't want to risk another embarrassment, so they're sending us first. And, it turns out, El Gato is an old acquaintance of mine."

She tapped the screen. "They should've sent me the file last night. This is a lot to absorb on short notice. Up until an hour ago, I thought I was resolving database server conflicts today."

"Also, the target and I were lovers."

"You...okay."

Manny grinned into his Yeti of coffee. "El Gato is a woman."

"Oh. That makes more... Not that I—"

"Also, my codename is Sinatra."

"Seriously?"

"Read, Beck. We got a full day."

11

Manny and Beck exited their vehicles at the same time and closed their car doors together. They were at a nondescript warehouse off Plantation in north Roanoke. Only one other car in the parking lot.

"I haven't finished reading," she said. "Why did El Gato invite you to dinner?"

"I don't know. Lover's revenge, perhaps? Torture?"

"I wish. How did she contact the DEA?"

Manny stopped at the unmarked door. "Ever since the DEA botched her arrest, she periodically taunts them through email." He grinned. "She's got style, no?"

Beck fished her credentials out from her jacket's breast pocket. "Even with top secret clearance, I've never been inside this warehouse. Access is based strictly on need. Let's see..."

She raised her government identification to the laser scanner. The device beeped and the door unlocked.

"This Supremacy License has teeth," she said.

Manny pulled the door for her and then entered into a

dark room requiring a retinal scan. They peered into the viewer and their names displayed on the screen. A moment later, the heavy interior door was pushed open by the sentry.

He greeted them, "Agents." He held a large PDA in his hand, their information and photographs displayed. "Welcome."

Manny nodded. "You work alone?"

"We maintain a five-person rotation, sir. At the moment, I'm here alone, yes." He led them into a large space like a workshop surrounded by bizarre tools and shelves and supply closets. Like a library for gadgets. "We don't innovate or manufacture here. I test the devices we're sent and store them for future use. You two are the first Supremacy Licenses we've ever had."

Manny scanned the room, pleased with the American exceptionalism on display.

"I need a few things," said Beck.

The man gestured to a console. "All yours."

Their voices sounded unnaturally hushed in the airtight area. Beck punched information into a computer and the sentry/engineer retrieved her requests. He set vacuum sealed boxes on the futuristic blue workbench.

"Is that all?" the man asked. "I'm in the next room, you need me." He left.

"We're on a clock so I'm thinking on the fly. Based on available intel, the security at the Palace is extremely impressive. We're getting creative." Beck opened the smaller box and held up a tiny device. Reminded Manny of a tick. "They'll scan you but this should remain undetected. The transmitter produces output only when you speak. There's no battery—it runs off body heat. Sensors inside register vibrations and I track the vibrations remotely, and my software codifies it into noise. I'll hear everything you say. There's no speaker but I can send pulses to communicate with you through Morse code."

"It's a mic that only hears me?"

"Yes. And if you remain silent, it doesn't transmit. Should foil the scanners, which they'll have and use. Have a seat," she said and he sat on the stool. Using small tweezers, she carefully inserted the black dot into his ear canal where his body heat provided an abundance of power. Even looking closely, the device was hard to detect. "One sec," she whispered. "The adhesive needs pressure to activate."

He enjoyed her breath on his neck.

She whispered, "Does it make you nervous? Me this close?"

"Beck, are you a virgin?"

Her hand twitched. "None of your business, Agent Sinatra."

"Then don't whisper into my ear. You got long legs. Did you run track in high school?"

"Cross country."

He sighed. "Thought so."

She backed away and clamped a headset around her ears. She depressed a trigger and Manny's right ear received a pleasant thumping noise. He interpreted the code—*say something.*

"Your Morse is rusty."

She removed the headset. "Perfect. You come through clear. This device ranges up to five miles."

"Fascinating. Like witchcraft. How do you know this stuff?"

"I'm NSA and collaborate with CIA and this isn't my

first rodeo with JFIC. Next." She held up a belt. "They'll make you take off your belt. But on the off chance they don't, this belt contains a video camera. It doesn't transmit though, so they'll see no outgoing signal. We'll download when you return."

Manny grimaced. "The buckle is gold. Do you have silver?"

"I do," she said, rummaging through the box. "Does it matter?"

"*Ay dios mio*, of course it matters, Beck."

She laid the silver-buckled belt onto the table. "An additional benefit to this belt. There is an inactive GPS locator built-in. It remains inactive until you rub your thumb across the back. The pressure and motion activate it. Handy in case you are kidnapped."

Manny snorted. Kidnapped.

"And one final device which could help at your dinner." She held up a tube of Chapstick. "A single-shot projectile device. Essentially, a gun with one bullet. The casing is plastic and so is the projectile. A metal detector registers nothing. There's gunpowder and a .22 slug. Aim and fire. And if questioned, you can take the top off— there's a small amount of real Chapstick to complete the disguise."

"One shot, and a .22 at that. A nearly useless tool."

"Just don't miss, Sinatra."

He grinned—he'd chosen his codename well.

"I'll park within five miles, close enough to monitor your ear mic," she said. "If things go poorly, I'll report your demise to Special Agent Weaver."

He nodded, enjoying the frissons and the trickle of adrenaline entering his veins. "This is going to be fun."

"I need an hour to pack my things." She reassembled the boxes and called for the sentry.

"And I need a place to change."

She asked, "How does one dress for a bizarre dinner with an international terrorist?"

"Trust me, Beck. I was made for this."

12

Manny cut loose on Interstate 81, southbound. His Camaro effortlessly crested 120 mph, leaving Noelle Beck in her unmarked government issue Ford far behind. Power hurtled through the engine and exhaust and he roared through the rising hills of southwest Virginia like on a weaving fighter jet.

The police officer who pulled him over suspected foul play, looking critically at Manny's outfit and car juxtaposed with his governmental credentials. However he spent one minute in his cruiser running the card through his database before hurrying back and apologizing with a pale face. Whatever the Supremacy License caused to pop up on his computer screen scared the hell out of him.

The Camaro bore him into the Appalachian Mountains near Gate City. He was forced to tap the shifter, lowering gears through the old mining towns.

Beck called him. He put it on speaker. She said, "For my previous assignment with JFIC, we had a week to prepare. Not four hours."

"Preparation is overrated. That's the marshal code. By

the way, when I catch her, marshals get top billing. Not the NSA. Write that down."

"This strikes me as a trap."

"That's why we're springing it."

"I need to verbally process this. If it's not a trap, what is it?" Her voice made his phone rattle in the cupholder.

"A date."

"You think?"

"Catalina and I planned to get married, before she left. But she's after more than just a reconnection."

"When did you last see her?"

Manny screwed up his eyes in thought. "Winter of 2010, maybe."

"Why did she leave?"

"Ay! You ask a lot of questions."

"We're partners," she said. "And I'm in the dark. Humor me."

"Her family was involved with the Honduran Congressional coup. They returned to consolidate their power."

"She was rich?"

"She was. I loved her and didn't try forcing her to change. I deliberately broke off ties but it appears she rose quickly through the Central American cartels."

Beck said, "No easy task in a world of brutal manhood."

"She's cunning and intelligent," said Manny with an affectionate smile. "Not to be underestimated."

"If something happens, coming to your aid will be difficult."

Uneasiness stirred in Manny's chest. Due to his upbringing he was more chauvinistic than his counterparts. He'd learned from experience his machismo was rarely welcome in this country, and he'd adapted as best he could. But Noelle Beck wasn't a deputy marshal. Despite her military background, currently she was a cyber security analyst or something—he should probably listen better. She'd been given an 1811 classification and a gun, but still he viewed her as the office computer technician, not someone who should be charging into danger.

Chauvinistic or not, he didn't want her hurt.

He said, "Don't you dare try. That's an order."

"You can't give me orders. You don't outrank me."

"Are you sure? I think I might."

"Here's something I don't understand—why would El Gato send a federal agency the address of the palace? That doesn't strike me as cunning or intelligent."

"From what I gather, the Appalachian Palace is not a secret. The owners are squeaky clean, you know? And the guests are wealthy and well connected. The result is like a loophole in the system. Busting in would create a legal nightmare and we'd probably lose. If we even *could* bust in."

"Sounds like base, when we were kids."

"Base?" asked Manny.

"You know, during a game of freeze tag. If you got to base, you were safe. Didn't you play tag?"

"When I was little, we stole from the vendors and fought with knives and boxed the bigger kids so they'd leave us alone. There were no safe places."

As he said it, unwelcome memories stirred. Like movie clips between his ears he couldn't turn off.

You're nothing.

You don't even know who you are.

Stop being a fool. She is dead.

He took a deep breath and pulled at his collar. Ay caramba. That happened fast.

Beck said something he missed. He scrambled backwards to remember her question—

"Good grief, Sinatra. Where'd you grow up?"

"I left Argentina when I was one and we moved to Compton. In 1986, I was two and President Ronald Regan gave me and two million other immigrants citizenship, so I'm American. I had my middle name legally changed to Ronald, by the way, when I was twenty-one. But my mom, she didn't qualify because of her record. She got deported when I was three and I went too. We moved around for the next fourteen-odd years before returning to Los Angeles."

"I didn't know. As a result, you have a heightened appreciation for this country."

"Bingo."

"Are you emotionally prepared to arrest your girlfriend?"

"Not yet."

"Sinatra—"

"I'm working on it."

13

Manny drove deep into the mountainous wilderness, civilization discarded in his rearview. He saw the appeal of building a retreat here—extreme isolation. Abandon all hope, ye who enter. The hills grew thick with unchecked green. He lowered the window to breathe it in—fertile undergrowth and humidity filled his car.

The email gave instructions to look for an unmarked drive next to the flagpole with an American flag at half-mast. Manny approved the reference point. At 5:55pm, he found it off Route 510 and turned without hesitation up the drive.

Some men run from danger. Some run towards. Manny had always sprinted directly into its teeth, driven by a heady combination of confidence and a withering disdain for consequence. As long as he didn't dwell on the past, he had an abundance of both.

"Located compound," he said out loud.

Around a bend, hidden from the main road, a security gate barred his path, supported by concrete pillars. The stone wall ran into the distance on each side.

Two men emerged. The first man walked around his car with a device, like a bizarre metal detector, scanning. Manny buzzed down his window to speak with the second man.

"Evening," said the sentry, dressed in tactical fatigues. "Think maybe you took a wrong turn."

"I'm on the guest list, amigo."

"Name?"

"Manuel Martinez."

Without replying, the man returned to his post beyond the fence. Manny resisted the urge to wink at the dual security cameras. The sentry finished with his electronic inspection and stepped away.

In his ear, the device thumped—*All is well?*

"Mmhm," he murmured quietly.

The man remerged from the fence and said, "I have a guest list with exactly one invitee. And you're it, Mr. Martinez."

"Means I'll have to carry the party."

"Have a pleasant evening, *amigo*." He stepped back and the gate smoothly retracted.

Manny drove a mile into the compound, winding upwards through pine and oak. Through the trees he saw a herd of deer grazing in a meadow. Did the guests hunt? He was positive the man planted a monitoring device on his Camaro so he didn't attempt further communication with Beck.

He reached the inner security wall. Black barricade poles lowered into the ground and he drove into a spacious cobbled courtyard. Ahead of him rose the palace proper, constituted by three levels of titanic windows and beige brickwork. Palace was an appropriate word. A fountain gurgled in the middle of the drive, encouraging traffic to move in a counter clockwise direction around it. Water lilies bobbed in the basin. Service trucks sat at the far end of the stones. Ahead of him, a motorcade of Toyota and luxury SUVs awaited employment, empty at the moment. A gardener used a spray hose to water exotic potted plants lining the courtyard. Sentries were stationed on the outer walls.

Two men waited for him near the doors. The first appeared to be one of the Palace's stewards, a kind-looking man in his sixties. He wore khakis, a blue jacket, and a white belt. The second man, Manny recognized. He didn't remember the name or details, but he knew the guy had been with Catalina in Los Angeles. The muscle. Tall, bulky, Hispanic, shaved head. Eyes set too far apart.

His ear pulsed. *Good luck, Sinatra.*

He eased to a stop at the entrance. The steward opened his door. Manny stood, slid into his ivory jacket, fastened the top button, and shook the man's proffered hand.

"Good evening, Mr. Martinez. I trust you found our home in the hills easily enough? My name is Hubert and I welcome you to the Appalachian Palace."

Manny cocked an eyebrow. "Appalachian Palace. Clever name."

"We've long been aware what the suspicious government calls our lodging." Hubert smiled, cagey, like sharing an inside joke. He spoke with easy manners and crisp punctuation. "And to be honest, I like the title."

Manny took in a deep breath and got hints of pine and early summer flora. "You own the place, Hubert?"

"I manage it. Our ownership is...complex. Please, come out of the sun and be refreshed."

Hubert led Manny into the shade of the vast house's

awning. A young woman met him and presented a silver bowl with a hot towel. Hubert's daughter? Grand daughter? Manny obliged, wiping his hands with it and came away smelling like lemons.

"This stalwart gentleman is Julio." Hubert indicated the tall Hispanic man. "One of our guests."

Manny said, "Buenas noches, Julio. De dónde vienes?"

- *Where are you from?* -

Julio kept his thick arms crossed. "Sabes de dónde soy."

- *You know where I'm from.* -

"Honduras?" said Manny.

The man nodded. Kinda.

Manny inserted his hands into his trouser pockets. "You don't like me, Julio. Poor judgment on your part. Might get you hurt."

Julio remained stoic. And stupid, he thought. Clearly he met Manny at the door to impart a message—don't mess with us.

Manny cared little for threats.

Hubert let them into a towering vestibule cooled by breeze coming from the shade. The floor was travertine and another fountain churned here. Divans and settees arranged in sitting spaces. Dueling stairs led to upper levels, and below them Manny spied modern chandeliers in the far rooms. Classical music emanated from the corner.

Manny caught his own reflection in a mirror. Olive khakis, ivory jacket, pressed shirt and tie. Hair sculpted without being shiny. The outfit was slim fit and bordered on being too tight, finding that sublime manicured look so many men couldn't attain. Should he have worn socks with his loafers? No. Why tinker with perfection.

"Hubert, your house is sexy as hell," he said.

"Thank you. I've never heard it described thusly, but I agree with the sentiment." They paused at a security checkpoint, manned by two armed sentries. They dressed like Hubert but with assault rifles. Ruined the look. "A thousand pardons for the inconvenience, but I'm sure you understand. We are a private residence and take a great deal of precaution."

"Understood."

"Your phone, shoes, belt, and anything in your pockets must remain here. Then you'll be subjected to a scan, I'm afraid. At the far side, we'll provide you with fresh slippers and belt. And, of course, your weapons will be confiscated until you leave."

Manny didn't move. He kept his hands in his pockets. He swiveled to cast a glance at Julio. "Seems I'm outnumbered and have no choice."

Hubert smiled politely. Julio did not.

"However. I'm reluctant."

"Rules are rules, Mr. Martinez. And you're far more outnumbered than you realize."

"I'm here to meet Catalina García," said Manny. He felt Julio flinch. "You prove to me she's here and I will comply with your rules. I'll strip nude if you like."

Neither man moved, but they shared a look. The sentries watched Manny impassively.

In his ear, *Sounds tense. Be careful, Sinatra.*

He let ten seconds tick before saying, "Come on, gentleman. You know Catalina. Tall brunette Latina. Even prettier than your house. Had a nose job recently."

From inside the house, laughter bubbled over like music. A woman emerged beyond the staircase. Such a woman. Her hair fell like spun satin, brown dyed dirty blonde. Heart-shaped face. A natural arch to her eyebrows. Strong architecture in her features, confident smile. Time had been good to her; she still resembled Eva Mendes, he thought, but more organic. She wore a golden dress—the bodice was tight, as though made for her and it probably had been; the hem swished at her knees. Her high black strappy heels clicked, as a femme fatale's should.

"Manuel," she said, striding closer in that catwalk motion only confident and graceful woman achieve. "No one has dared mention my nose in three years."

"Cowards. I liked your old one better."

"Liar." In Spanish, she said, "The breasts are new too. Perhaps you want to insult them also?"

"I am a gentleman. Maybe later."

She came into his arms and kissed his mouth. With her heels, she was only two inches shorter. He embraced her and they stayed in that position, entirely insular, for half a minute. Friendly, affectionate, wary. Manny kept the torrent of emotions at bay, but only through discipline and a trickle of anger he let seep through. Anger as armor.

She stepped away. Cleared her throat. "It is good to see you, Manuel. I like your hair."

"Obviously."

"You must surrender your items to these nasty gentleman," she said and she undid his jacket button. "Here, I will help."

"Help me undress? If you insist."

In his ear, *Oh my.*

14

Catalina led him through a tour of the house. Not all of it, he knew, only the sections the stewards allowed. Hubert brought them champagne aperitifs as they investigated salons with leather settees and ottomans, and indoor gardens with jardinières and mosaic tiled walls.

She'd grown harder. Gone was the youthful buoyancy, the emanating optimism. Her energy took the form of determination now. Her eyes pierced instead of hoped. She wore self-possession like a crown. Yet she clung tightly to his free hand as they walked and Manny's long dormant affection erupted like a backdraft. He'd once loved this woman and he hadn't dared since, with anyone. Love was too great a cost to bear.

She wore no lipstick. For him? He always hated it. She now wore only mascara, other makeup unnecessary.

They strolled through the impressive labyrinth, the house even larger than it outwardly appeared. Julio followed everywhere, glaring.

Manny said in English, "Your henchman seems perturbed."

"He doesn't like you. He was on the plane when we left and had to listen to me cry. Plus, you are with the police." She shrugged a shoulder, which he found charming. "So..."

Manny called over his shoulder, "Ay, chupacabra, I'll behave. Give the lady and me privacy, *sí*?" They moved down the hall and Julio followed. "You are warned."

They were also tailed by two other guards, who kept a respectful distance.

Catalina led him into a library and she pointed at a turbulent painting on the wall. "An original Thomas Hart Benton, from the 1920s. Henry Hill brought it during a stay, decades ago. He worked with the Lucchese crime family."

Manny sipped his champagne and set the flute down. "How do you know?"

"I received the same tour you're on. And I find American organized crime more interesting than my country's. The cruelty is more...tasteful. It's something of a tradition, at this house, that guests leave a gift."

"What did you bring?"

"Tuberose bulbs, from the executive garden of Honduras."

Manny didn't reply. He pivoted smoothly and kicked Julio between the legs. A snap kick, making solid contact through his slippers. His target's face went purple and he emitted a strained hissing. Manny knew the feeling—an overwhelming agony, incapable of being shrugged off. Julio slumped to the ground.

"Now." He retrieved his flute. "Cheers. To privacy."

Catalina wore a wicked smile, as though pain was a guilty pleasure. "You still fight dirty."

"Not dirty. Efficient. He was warned." He offered her an arm and they left the library and its prone occupant.

"He will get revenge, Manuel. And I cannot stop him."

"Your mission in Honduras went well?"

"Ten years ago? The coup was a success. We used our new congressional influence to arrange contracts with traffickers around the world. Hired enough local warlords for protection and underbid the old guard."

"Trafficking narcotics."

"I wish you had joined us. It was a costly mess and very bloody. We could have used you." She squeezed his bicep. "You'd be rich now."

"You're the only Honduran export I give a damn about. Keep your money."

"The business is hard. My brothers began dying, so I married into another family to bring peace."

"All your brothers are dead?" asked Manny.

"No. I still have one. And other family, like Julio."

"And your husband?"

"He was murdered."

"Who killed him?"

Her lips twisted, a tight angry smile. "A lady never tells."

Goosebumps on his arms. She killed her own husband? Good hell, what happened to the girl he knew in Los Angeles?

She continued, "I quit the drug trade years ago, after your Drug Enforcement Agency got too close."

"They send you their best."

"Yes." She squeezed him again, walking close enough that he felt the heat she emanated. "They did."

In his ear he heard pulses. *Your side of the conversation is fascinating.*

Manny took a deep breath to mask the pause as he listened. "I'm not DEA."

"I know. I watch your career with interest from afar. Your talents are wasted in your position, Manuel."

"I enjoy what I do."

"So?"

"It matters. To me."

"Working for the American government."

"Democracy is one of the bright lights keeping evil at bay."

She laughed softly through her nose. "You don't believe that. You are too violent and raw. Roanoke's not even a very big city. And you live with another man."

"Mack August. He's my friend."

"I remember Mackenzie. Why did you follow him to the East Coast?"

"I had to get out. My soul was becoming ruined. Ten years running vice in south L.A. is enough. I got in my car and drove and ended up here. Life gave me three things to keep the hate away. Friendship, my career, and a love for America. It's not much, I know. And it sounds absurd. But it's what I cling to."

"Yet it's still not enough. Is it," she said, and her words didn't form a question. "I know the feeling. Our youthful idols falling flat. Some nights I pray I won't wake up."

"You'll get your wish if you don't quit the lifestyle."

They were underground now. Tucked away from sophisticated surveillance. She paused at a double-door entrance. "I believe it's dinner time. Hungry?"

"What's on the menu?"

She smiled again. Her teeth were perfect and brilliant. "Come sit. The company is worth the risk."

The dining room was grand, lit with a panoply of

candles. A long oaken table stood in the middle on rich crimson carpet. A place for her at one end and his at the other. The scent of freshly baked bread filled the room.

They entered and the hairs on Manny's neck stood. He felt, rather than heard, a high-pitched whine. A short burst that made him shiver. The small microphone in his ear short-circuited, burning him. A tiny mark but inside his ear canal it hurt. Badly.

Catalina watched for any reaction. Manny showed nothing. He asked, "Did you feel something?"

"Oh yes, I should have warned you. This room is protected with small electromagnetic pulses at the doors. I hope you weren't carrying electronics."

"They were taken from me," he said. "A damn suspicious group, you criminals."

He was now alone in the wolf's den.

Poor Beck. She would be near a cardiac episode.

They moved to the long table. He pulled the chair for her, waited until she sat, and moved to his place.

He gestured at the arrangement. "We're eight feet apart."

"It's tradition."

He grabbed his plate and silverware and flute, and returned to her. He set a new place at the high-backed chair immediately to her right. "A stupid tradition."

"Always the rule breaker, Manuel. Even as a cop."

He took off his jacket and draped it neatly on the adjacent chair. He popped the cork from the chilled bottle of champagne, filled her glass, and sat.

"Dom Pérignon Brut," he noted.

"The very best for you."

"Never tried it. Coffee and champagne, the two things America can't do."

Julio returned, the pain of his injuries abated enough to allow full movement. He stood in the corner, near another Hispanic sentry. A few more minutes and he'd be healthy enough to cause trouble.

She said, "You're taller than I remember. Also I do not recall you being so...cultured."

"What was I?"

"A mess. A handsome one."

He winked "I'm still there. But I stuck out, so I became a gentleman. Or learned to fake it. Became the best American I could."

"After I left."

"I needed it. Needed to be something other than a fighter."

"Americans are fat and lazy," she pointed out.

"I'm the *best* kind of American. Not one who takes it for granted."

Switching effortlessly into Spanish, she asked, "That is why you drive the absurd car?"

"Careful how you speak about the Camaro, *mujer*. It's American as Elvis."

"You hate Elvis."

"Then it's American as Frank Sinatra."

"You said the right kind of American. Isn't a muscle car...beneath you?"

Servers came, bringing hot bowls of gazpachuelo soup.

Manny raised his glass to her, ceding the point. "Us Americans, we don't make elegant cars. Besides, I enjoy the horsepower."

"Maybe a Cadillac?"

"A Corvette, soon as I get a raise."

"Come with me, Manuel." She clinked her glass

against his. "I will make you rich. You can buy a fleet of American cars."

He didn't respond to her offer. Was it genuine? They ate their soup, followed by salad. The food was exquisite; he told the servers so.

Despite his best efforts, they fell under each other's spell and the enchantment of halcyon memories. Old longings flared.

His mouth watered when plates of pozole were set in front of them. He hadn't seen this dish since he was a boy. Before he could try, Julio spoke.

"Catalina. I am done waiting. I will deal with the American cop here or outside. *Now*."

Manny set down his silverware. He asked, "Julio is your family?"

"Cousin. I'm afraid you deserve what's coming, Manuel. I learned from experience—don't interfere in the petty disputes of men."

"What if I kill him?"

She was breathing deeply and her rich brown eyes took on greater sparkle. The desire echoed his own. She said, "He's not my favorite cousin."

"*Bien.* I'll make this quick, one way or another. I want dessert."

"You boys and your insecurities ruin everything." Though she sounded pleased.

Manny pushed back his chair, stood, and set his napkin on the table.

Julio didn't wait; furious, he attacked Manny in the dining room. Taller than Manny, and heavier, confident of easy victory, throwing punches. Manny in a forward stance, natural for him, a little stiff, deflecting the rights, wary of any big left. Child's play.

Hubert hurried in. "Gentlemen! We have rules for this."

Manny slipped a punch, throwing a left into Julio's stomach and circling behind. Julio grunted in pain and surprise.

"Outside, Julio?" he asked. "For the sake of Hubert. Worried the feds will see your embarrassment on satellite?"

"*Puta!*"

"Fighting here feels like getting mud on a leather couch."

Julio caught him off guard, a short kick to his knee. Manny limped backwards. More punches now, Manny parrying, loosening, knees bent, left foot forward, catching the odd carom in his jaw but they were ineffectual. He was a marshal, after all—a professional absorber of punishment.

Julio was frustrated, unable to penetrate, accustomed to overwhelming lesser fighters, his size and strength more than enough to crush most men on the planet; he moved slowly and off balance.

Manny caught him hard on the nose and retreated again. Julio breathing heavy and eyes watering

"Don't stop now, boys," said Catalina.

Julio came on. Manny abandoned defense. Feinted a left jab. Hit him a right into the jaw. A powerful uppercut next under the chin. Enough to sunder most men and it bruised Manny's hand, but Julio only staggered like an oak.

Disaster, then. The nearby Hispanic sentry hit Manny from behind. A cheap shot. Felt like a crisp blow from the butt of an assault rifle, hard enough to daze him. Manny, lights blinking, a realization he'd fallen to the floor. The fight's balance was drastically altered by the second assailant.

"Nicolás!" shouted Catalina.

Manny rolling away, trying to recalibrate the spinning gyroscope between his ears. Nicolás, the sentry, struck him another blow. The butt of his weapon cut open Manny's eyebrow.

Manny kicking at the man, trying to rise, but Julio hit him—an open handed slap against the ear. Tremendously painful, Manny's whole head ringing.

From behind, Julio hauled him up. Manny's arms pinned. He tried to kick Nicolás again but missed and, helpless, received a strong chop to his abdomen. Grunting in pain.

From a distance he heard Catalina's voice. Words drowned out by thunder in his ears.

"Again," said Julio, nearly wrenching Manny's arms out of socket. Julio using a snarling voice. "In the groin."

"Two against one?" wheezed Manny. "Make it fair. Call a few more of your friends."

Nicolás raising the assault rifle, prepared to inflict violent harm on Manny's genitals.

Manny squirming, his arms held fast. At the last second he plunged forward. Julio pulled off balance. Falling, both of them. Nicolás missed, connecting with Julio's shoulder instead.

The sounds of pain and exertion bouncing and clashing against the dignified air of the dining room.

Manny up first, shoving Nicolás, who'd gotten too close. He kicked Julio in the face, busting his teeth, and grabbed the top rail of a high-backed chair. He swung it like a ponderous club, catching Nicolás off balance. The exquisitely fine chair cracked against the sentry's head

Hubert made a groaning noise—each chair cost five thousand dollars.

Nicolás wobbling. Manny snapped the broken back off the chair and he brought the hard seat crashing onto the sentry's skull. The wood split and Nicolás fell.

Breathing heavy, bleeding from forehead and ear, he turned to Julio. He tore off the chair's broken armrest and, using it like a wooden dagger, drove it into Julio's shoulder. The big man roared. Clutching the jagged shard and toppling.

At the table, Catalina saying something he couldn't hear.

Manny knelt on Julio's chest. Hit him in the nose again and shoved the makeshift wooden dagger further into Julio's meaty muscle. The shoulder looked ruined and would require surgery. "I don't like warnings. You're alive for the sake of your cousin."

Julio, unable to respond, eyes bulging.

Manny got up. Panting. His blood running hot and he'd grown tunnel vision. He retrieved the sentry's fallen assault rifle. An AK-12. He crouched beside Nicolás and shoved the barrel of the rifle into the sentry's mouth.

Nicolás gagging. Dazed and concussed. The barrel clicked against his teeth, pressed against his tongue.

"That wasn't your fight, amigo," said Manny. "Never hit a man from behind. We're a civilized people."

Manny trembling with rage—a rising tide. He pushed off the gun's safety.

"I kill you, the fight is over. I let you live? Maybe the others don't get the message. You understand."

Nicolás's breath hissed raggedly through his nose. Manny squeezed the trigger.

"Manuel," said Catalina.

Manny caught a note of warning in her voice. His finger paused and he glanced up. Eight guards—three Hispanic, and five with Hubert—stood in a circle. Weapons trained on him.

"It's *over*, Manuel. You won. Get up." Catalina stood at the table. At the moment she wore the airs of a cartel boss, not his elegant date.

"Outnumbered, eh?"

Hubert gave him a small nod and gestured to the ruined men and broken chair. His face looked hard—he'd ordered guests eliminated before and he'd do it again if necessary. "Indeed. The fight is concluded. I insist."

Manny stood. The wrath passed like a storm. He set the safety again and laid the rifle on the table. His pozole was still warm. Dipping his napkin into ice water, Manny dabbed at his forehead and ear. Somehow his lip bled too. "Dammit," he said. "My shirt is ripped."

Catalina's anger passed too. Replaced by something else, equally passionate. She took his hand. Her eyes were wide, her skin flushed. She glanced at Hubert. "We'll take the rest of our dinner in my bedroom. Later."

"Very good."

"Don't forget dessert," Manny told the steward. "The devil may care, as long as I'm eating carbs."

Manny grabbed the bottle of Dom Pérignon as Catalina dragged him from the room.

15

Manny inspected his eyebrow and lip in the mirror the following morning. Both were swollen and bruised.

Catalina's bedroom was at least twenty feet underground and July's morning sunlight reflected in via a system of mirrors through the ceiling.

She sat shamelessly naked on the bed, reclining against pillows. Desire uncoiled in his chest again, watching her reflection. Their night had been vigorous and consuming, if less prolonged than in their twenties.

Probably not how Weaver envisioned this going.

Catalina's finger idly traced her phone's screen, scanning messages. He missed his phone. And his firearms. And his coffee.

She said, "Your agencies must be beside themselves, wondering why I returned."

"Why did you?"

"To be ravaged by the most handsome man alive."

He watched her through the mirror. "Part of the service us marshals provide."

"The last I saw you, you didn't have this many tattoos. Or scars."

"I got aggressive. Turns out, neither fill the void."

"The designs, what do they symbolize?"

"Damned nonsense, I think, looking back."

Her quarters had the look of a well-furnished Bed and Breakfast guest room, as opposed to a hotel. A large painting of pine trees, probably original and probably stolen, dominated the opposite wall.

She asked, "Do your police lie in wait outside my doors?"

"No."

"They won't catch me."

He chuckled. "They want this done peacefully."

"They hope I'll surrender?"

Instead of replying, he grimly eyed the coffee mug set next to the mirror. Without his nutritional additives, the stuff tasted like weak gruel. He'd grown spoiled.

"Come with me, Manuel. I no longer traffic narcotics. I'm a power broker now."

"Did you help destabilize the Honduran currency in 2017?"

She smiled, pleased. "I did. And I bought a large percentage of the banana exports, which, believe it or not, helped us influence the Brazilian election. You can't imagine the power that crop yields."

"Honduras is a mess."

"A disaster."

"Because of you," he said, fighting off a sense of vertigo. That girl on the tarmac at the airport in Los Angeles. What the hell happened to her?

"Partly. But I profited, the American equivalent of seventy-five million."

"Impossible."

"The amount of money surging through the world still takes my breath, Manuel."

"Why are you in America, Catalina? What's worth the risk?"

She held his eyes in the reflection. "I told you. My nights are dark and cold. Often I hope I won't wake. I'm here for the only man I love."

"That's not all."

"It is. I will make you rich."

"I have enough."

She crossed her arms over her stomach. "Last night, you beat Julio and Nicolás in an unfair fight. Professional hitmen. I see the rage in you, Manuel. You need this. And I know *dozens* of men who need to be killed with dining room chairs. Or anyway you prefer. I'll pay you a million each."

"A *million*."

A glint in her eye. "A million *each*. We'll watch the video tapes of your work and you'll carry me to bed after."

"*Guau*."

"Yes."

"Do you think I'm a fool? You didn't come for just me." Although, even as he said it, he wondered. He knew the power of loneliness, of loss.

"Why else would I return to this forsaken part of Virginia?"

"Kentucky."

"Who cares. My husband died years ago. I've been alone since."

"What country do you plan on destroying next?"

"If I tell you, will you inform your government?"

"I might."

She laughed, a warm and mocking sound. "Stay with me. We'll fly out in a few days and I'll tell you everything. Please, Manuel. Your life can begin again. But right now, there is only the immediate."

He turned from the mirror. Picked up his mug and sipped the coffee. Yuck. He pointed at her with the hand holding the cup. "I like them, by the way."

"Like what?"

"Your surgical enhancements. You asked if I wanted to insult them, earlier. I don't."

Her mouth twisted in a tight smile. "I'm glad you approve. Very little about me is authentic. A price I pay for wealth."

"There is no price worth your soul." He set down the coffee. "But you sold that already, I think."

"I'll buy another."

"Mine?"

Her toes pushed at the sheet. "We'll share. Now take off those pants and return to my bed."

"I have to go."

"My guards won't let you."

"It'll take all of them to stop me," he said, but it was pure bravado. He didn't take much convincing to stay. Just the sight of her. He wasn't proud of his weakness and he imagined she used similar methods to weave her webs in Central America. The thought twisted his stomach with hurt.

She said, "One hour more. Then you must go, and tell your agencies how wicked I am. But I bet you'll leave a few details off your report."

He approached her side of the bed. "How dare you. I am a professional."

"Not for much longer, my love."

16

Ten Years Earlier

IN THE BACKYARD of a small ranch on Palmer Street in Compton, Manny and Catalina sat at a picnic table. There was no lawn, only a dirt patch scoured by large pit bulls. The chain fence needed replacing, held together in spots by bent coat hangers.

Two charcoal grills sizzled near the house and ten of Catalina's extended family milled near the stereo. Angry music thumped, forcing them to raise their voices.

Manny and Catalina chatted with Scotty, the owner of the ranch. He said, "I heard you bust my neighbor."

Manny inclined his head, which was shaved. "Maybe. Who?"

"Little Kevin. Little Kevin with only one foot. Three houses up."

"*Sí.* I forgot. Little Kevin beats up kids, *migo*. And does worse than that. Then makes them sell crack at Tucker Park. Felt good, busting his ass."

Catalina smiled at Manuel, clinging tightly to his arm with her free hand. Manuel, her boyfriend. Soon to be fiancé, she hoped. She'd fallen for him immediately last year, the quiet brooding man, angry at the world—for all of his hurt and rage, he softened when he looked at her. True, he was a cop, but a cop she could control. Plus, never had a man been so perfectly crafted.

He saw the smile. Winked at her.

Scotty was high and he turned red eyes onto Catalina. "You dating a badge, huh. Gettin' that bacon."

Her back stiffened. At twenty-five, she was the pinnacle of health and cash and privilege. So breathtaking, thought Manny, looking away took discipline. She didn't belong in this backyard. Or this life.

"I date who I want to date, Scotty."

"Does Raf know?"

"He knows I'm dating Manuel."

"But does he *know*? Does Raf know your boy's bacon?"

Catalina paused. Her older brother ran their enterprise since the death of her father. Not a man to trifle with. She set down her bottle of Coca-Cola—she insisted the American recipe was superior to the Honduran. "Rafael is meeting Manuel today."

"Oh shit," said Scotty. "In my backyard? You gonna kill a cop in my backyard?"

Most of the guests eavesdropped on their conversation. They represented various levels of drug distribution throughout Compton, locally affiliated with MS-13. Catalina's boyfriend was an issue. They knew he wasn't a Boy Scout and that he looked the other way for Catalina's sake. But he wasn't in their pocket either. The rumors surrounding Manuel Martinez were legendary—one of the cops gangsters truly feared.

Scotty had a complex situation brewing in his backyard and he didn't like it.

Manny grinned. "Killing me in your backyard gets you some street cred, Scotty."

"I got street cred, mang."

"Not the streets I work. Mang."

Catalina squeezed his hand. "Manuel, we are his guest. Behave."

Overhead, a perfect blue. Sunlight streamed in, fresh and golden.

Scotty leaned back. Relit his joint stub, inhaled, and held it. When he spoke, green smoke leaked out of his nose and mouth. "What'cha gonna do, cop? When your girl leaves?"

"Leaves?"

"You can't hear? Yeah leaves."

Manny glanced at her. "*Qué?* What's he talking about?"

"He's...I..." she said, caught off guard.

Scotty cackled. "She ain't told you!"

"I...I haven't yet. Because, well, I don't know what will happen." She was turning a shade of red.

"You're leaving?"

"No! Maybe. I don't know. Rafael says we need to return to Honduras."

A muscle in Manny's jaw flexed. "For vacation."

"Or maybe longer."

"Longer."

The earth tilted under Manny's feet. Foundations, firm for months, suddenly quaked. The photograph he kept in his pocket seemed to burn. He tried to speak and couldn't. His heart ached and fingers tingled.

Could old fears spark this quickly? Was his past buried so shallow? All his training, years spent fighting, his strict disciplinary regiment, his meditations, his diet, his military education, his career, his hard work, all of it suddenly powerless at the first sign of abandonment.

He cleared his throat and tried again. "You're leaving."

"I want you to come with us. I was going to ask you."

"You didn't."

"But I will! I'm not like the bitch in that picture you carry."

He didn't believe her. Couldn't believe her.

Manny stood. Grabbed the table for support. The world blurred. Scotty laughed at him and so did the woman in the photograph.

She was abandoning him.

"I have to go," he said.

"But you haven't met Rafael yet!"

Manny was already moving toward his car, lost.

17

Manny asked, "When do you leave?"

Catalina smiled. They stood at the top of the stairs, near the entrance. She took hold of his jacket by the lapels and tugged. "I'm only kicking you out because I have business calls to make, death warrants to sign, that kind of thing. Otherwise I'd look at you all day. Such a handsome man. They don't make men like this in Honduras. I leave soon. And you're coming with me."

"To where?" He took her hand and kissed it.

"Manuel. Quit playing games. You're going to lose me again. Do you understand? I'm not staying. Your police cannot catch me. I'll be gone. You won't know where. And you'll be alone once more."

"Catalina—"

"No. Don't speak. Think. You have a few more days to decide. Clearly I cannot stay in America. Your agencies track my every move."

His mind scrambled for other ways to get information. Any way to stall his departure. "If I join you, what would I do? I'm no man of leisure."

"I have enemies. As I said, a million for each head you bring me. I'll tell you more once we're in the air. *Hasta luego, mi alma.* " She turned and went down the hallway. He steeled his nerve, forced himself to feel nothing, to say nothing, and he slowly descended the staircase. Alone.

Hubert met him at the bottom. "I hope you enjoyed your stay, Mr. Martinez."

"More than I thought possible."

"May I show you one more thing, before you go?" Hubert turned without waiting and led him through the house to rooms off limits before. Past the vast kitchen and into the utilitarian wing. Manny's steps faltered, only for a half second, as he caught sight of an armory. An imposing room, inlaid neatly with assault rifles, and rocket launchers, and ammunition, and explosives. He also saw barracks, two long rooms with bunk beds.

Manny was being shown this intentionally. Sending a message to the entirety of the American law enforcement —don't try it.

He brought Manny to a northern window wall, overlooking Kentenia State Forest. An undisturbed carpet of green trees to the horizon.

"A beautiful view, don't you think?" asked Hubert.

Below them, two dozen men drilled under the careful eye of a sergeant. Three helicopters were visible from this angle, covered by a retractable roof.

Manny noted, "Very impressive, yes."

"Vistas like this bring me peace. Assures me that the world is wide and clean and properly ordered."

"That reminds me. Thank you for repairing my shirt. The seam is perfect."

"Of course, Mr. Martinez."

"The shirt is American, you noted."

Hubert smiled. "As Ms. Catalina says, nothing but the best for you."

"Your staff is larger than I thought," he said, nodding to the yard below and the men currently doing push-ups.

"This house serves many functions. One of which is rehabilitation. When members of the American military are discharged without honor, and done so unjustly, we sometimes reach out to these soldiers and offer them a place to live. In exchange for their services, of course."

"I understand."

"I hope so."

"Where is Catalina going, Hubert? When she leaves here?"

"Honestly, I have no idea. That is not my business. And to be frank nor is it yours. I hope you'll visit again, Mr. Martinez." Hubert turned from the window and bowed, saying goodbye. "Give us a day's notice and we're happy to accommodate you."

Manny shot Hubert with his finger. "You got it."

"The security detail will return your items as you depart. Have a pleasant day."

Manny went back the way he came, his head buzzing from the unofficial deal he'd just struck; keep your mouth closed about this place and there will be no trouble. And potentially, he thought, some of the underworld's services were just availed to him.

He passed the barracks and down the intersecting hallway he noticed Nicolás. The sentry from last night— he saw Manny and moved out of sight quickly, and Manny continued walking.

He expected this. Catalina's security retinue had a bone to pick. Julio was humiliated and couldn't simply let Manny walk.

From his pocket, he fished out Beck's tube of Chapstick. He twisted the bottom and the device clicked.

A nearly useless tool, he'd told her.

However...

As he approached the front vestibule, Julio himself stepped out of the kitchen. His right arm held by a sling. In his left fist, he gripped a pistol.

A duel to the death then. He planned to kill Manny without a word spoken.

Clearly Julio was right handed. He held the pistol unnaturally and his aim was slow. The half second delay he required to bring the pistol to bear saved Manny's life.

He stepped into Julio, beyond the barrel of the man's pistol. Pressed the Chapstick tube firmly into the fleshy crease where jaw met throat, above the Adam's apple. Aimed upward at the brain. Pressed the button.

The tube flashed and partially melted, singeing Manny's fingertips. Sounded like a weak firecracker. Julio stiffened and his eyes went cross, gazing faraway.

Manny didn't break stride, nor even remove his left hand from his trouser pocket.

"*Adios, mijito,*" he said.

How far would a .22 slug penetrate from the esophagus? Into the brain, it appeared. Would Julio die? Or merely suffer permanent and debilitating brain damage? He didn't care, one way or another.

Sometimes warnings simply didn't work.

A minute later, Hubert's security detail politely returned his shoes, belt, phone, and firearms.

18

"Sinatra, thank God," said Beck.

Manny drove away from the house, talking on speaker. "Are you allowed to say that?"

"Of course. I'm speaking literally. Are you injured?"

"I'm fine. An EMP broke the mic. Where are you?"

"A hotel in Gate City."

"*Qué susto!* Gate City's over an hour away."

"It's the closest I could find. I waited until two in the morning before driving here," she said. "I assumed you died, Sinatra."

No complaint about her hotel selection was appropriate, he supposed. Especially recalling what he'd been doing late the previous evening.

"I'm sure my car is bugged. Go back to sleep. I'll get a room and meet you later today. Our target isn't going anywhere. Yet."

"You found her, then."

"She's there," he said.

Though he still didn't know why. Or how to arrest her. Or if he even could force himself to.

AT NOON, he and Beck sat in his Camaro wearing Bluetooth ear pieces connected to his phone. Across the street, a 7-Eleven sign buzzed noisily and locals bought cheap snacks.

JFIC's director, Special Agent Weaver, spoke directly into their ears. "This line is encrypted but his hardware might be compromised."

"It was," said Manny. "Beck discovered two bugs, removed both, updated the SIM card, and swapped out circuitry."

Beck didn't bother to correct his cybersecurity jargon. "Close enough. I also removed a magnetic GPS tracking device from his car."

"Give me the short version, Sinatra."

"She's there. El Gato."

"Bingo. What's she doing?"

"She wouldn't say. She no longer traffics narcotics, preferring to topple governments instead. From context clues, I think another country is on her agenda."

"You had no chance at extraction?"

"None."

"Figured. We didn't expect you to storm the castle and shoot your way out. What'd she want?"

"To reconnect. She wants me to leave with her. To be a hired hitman, essentially. And to share her bed."

Weaver released a vexed sigh. "JFIC's newest agent, the paramour of an international terrorist."

Manny made a shrugging motion. "Can't blame the poor girl."

Weaver asked, "That's the only reason she's here?"

"No. There's something else. I'm still working on it."

"What's your impression of the Palace?"

"It's better than you know. Guests sleep deep underground. Bunker-buster missiles would do the trick."

"On American soil? No chance."

"The security team is large, maybe twenty-five," he said and Weaver made a surprised noise. "All ex-military. Plus El Gato's personal detail. Impressive arsenal. The house hides choppers and a fleet of SUVs. They gave me glimpses only. But I saw infrared cameras, motion sensors, rocket launchers, barricades, reinforced walls and windows."

She whistled. "They intentionally let you see? A warning, then."

"Probably. You'd need Kentucky's National Guard to knock it down."

Weaver said, "And they know we don't want that political nightmare. Type up an FD-302 and make recommendations. I need to touch base with our board of supervisors. Catching her would be a serious feather in the cap."

He didn't respond. He gazed at the 7-Eleven sign and the picture went fuzzy. Little Catalina, drinking a Coke. Crying on the airplane. Locked behind bars, a feather in the cap of the DEA.

Weaver said, "It's Tuesday, Sinatra. That private jet leaves Saturday morning from Roanoke Airport. I need your report tonight."

19

"I sprained my ankle during basic training," said Beck. "Night maneuvers. We went alone and they gave us a canteen and a compass and I stepped in a hole during the first mile. I made it to the end, limping and hopping, but I was last. The worst night of my life. Yesterday came close, though, thinking my partner was dead."

Sinatra took her trauma as a compliment.

They sat at a private table at the town's only true bar. Fake paneling on the walls, a television turned to ESPN and the other to Fox News, pictures of local high school football on the walls. The bartender, a gorilla of a man with heavy forearms, judged them foreign and suspicious.

Beck drank a Sprite. Nothing with alcohol or caffeine.

Manny sipped his whiskey sour, which was bad, and stewed. His laptop sat open on the table, glaring at him. Typing up his report clarified one major fact—he'd botched the job. No way around it. He'd lost his logic at the sight of her. The Julios and the Nicoláses and the Diegos and the Milos of the world didn't cause him worry. Nor did the Marshal Warrens or the Director Douglases or the Special Agent Weavers. Not even high ranking mobsters, like the District Kings. But one look at Catalina García...

He should have attempted extraction in the middle of the night. Drugged her, carried her out, maybe. But that was worse than wishful thinking. Worse than revisionist history. Any attempt would've resulted in disaster.

Weaver had expressed no disappointment in his performance but only because she hadn't been watching his evening. He demanded better of himself.

He asked himself for the hundredth time, what *should* he have done differently?

Kept his pants on, for one.

Beck was speaking, her cheeks pink with passion. "It makes me mad. I'm not a field operative. I left the Air Force for a reason. Hidden off the highway, alone, listening to thousands of animals in the dark forest, assuming you'd been shot. I started thinking about the nature of JFIC and our assignment. And...it's asinine, sending two operatives *alone* to a place like that."

Manny nodded. It was an unusual and dangerous way to catch a fugitive. And yet, he loved it. He felt alive and free, away from rules and supervision. Even if he hadn't succeeded. Yet.

She continued, "You died. In my head, you were dead. I'd alert JFIC, and then I'd be transferred, and that would be that. No one at the Marshal's office would know what happened to you."

"Maybe not."

"It's outrageous. I'm in *cyber* security. I don't know why I agreed."

"We're doing good, Beck. Protecting the realm. Making the world a better place."

"I don't doubt the impetus, I doubt the methods."

"But we're having fun. Doesn't that count?"

"It does not. I'm angry."

He turned his eyes back to his screen.

The size of the hospitality staff and security force suggests the APOG is part of a larger structure. A 'franchise,' for lack of a better term, because it's too well organized and thorough to be the brainchild of one individual. The array of munitions alone indicates contacts within the military...

He scrolled down.

...recommend we prepare for a large security detail escorting El Gato to Roanoke's airport. (If indeed she utilizes the plane reserved by APOG) Evidence suggests she and her team will not surrender without using force to resist. Although she admitted she knows our agencies track her, she indicated we would not be able to apprehend her. Possibly due...

He leaned back and laced fingers across his abdomen. Glaring details were omitted from his FD-302. Such as, why was she here? And where was she going next?

Beck rested her chin in her palm and scowled at her laptop. Tapped a few keys. "I'm finding nothing. I'm mining databases and news articles for El Gato and Catalina García, focusing on Brazil and Honduras and banana crops, and...zip. Even with my security clearance. It's like the woman didn't exist for the past four years."

"Her husband died. Assassination. Approximately three years ago. A well-connected drug lord in Honduras, I assume. If we find him, we'll unearth her Honduran alias."

She nodded and her finger flew across the keys. "Worth a shot."

They drank in silence for ten minutes.

Eventually she asked, "Is it possible she's telling the truth? She's only here for you?"

"No. There's another reason."

"What's she like?"

Manny released a blast of air at the ceiling. "She's passionate. Driven. Hedonistic. Perhaps a little sadistic. Her father made a lot of money, so she's spoiled. But she's sentimental. Loyal to her family. Affectionate."

"Affectionate?"

Manny nodded. Drank some whiskey sour. Should've ordered a beer. He said, "Your little gun worked, by the way."

"The Chapstick tube?"

"One of her cousins got handsy. And maybe I behaved poorly and embarrassed him. It was me or him, and they'd taken my guns. So..."

Her eyebrows rose. "You killed him. Close range?"

He nodded. "It's quiet. Burnt my fingers."

"I'll put that in the files. I'm not sure if its ever been fired in the field."

"Fields," said Manny, irritated and changing the subject. "There's nothing near the Appalachian Palace except forests and *fields*. What the hell is she doing here? Why *here*? Why this place? Other than me."

"Maybe there's something about this particular area? Something we don't know." Beck opened Google Maps and zoomed in.

"There's nothing. Nada."

Beck surfed the geographic region and scanned local newspapers and articles. "Very little. Could she be here for the coal mines?"

"Not her style. She's into espionage and government secrets and blackmail."

The screen's light tinted her face blue. "Railroads?"

"No."

"Whiskey? Tobacco?" she asked, scrolling through the region's major employers. "Probably not. Maybe the prison at Big Stone Gap?"

"The prison?" Manny's drink paused halfway to his mouth.

"Wallens Ridge State Prison. Seven hundred inmates. Forty miles from the Appalachian Palace."

He set the drink down and drummed his fingers on the table. Interesting idea. But what would she want with the prison?

"Surely El Gato wouldn't try a jailbreak," she said.

"No. She doesn't want attention and that would wake the whole state. Even if she did, her crew is too small. And the Palace would never get its hands that dirty."

"Not much of value in a prison, anyway. What else—"

"Check for prisoners being released this week."

She sucked at her teeth and worked. "How on earth do I do *that?*" The question was for herself, not him.

Manny took the whiskey back to the bar and said, "This is piss."

The gorilla bartender eyed him coolly. "Too bad, no refunds."

"I don't want a refund. I want to pour this into your toxic waste bin."

"Think you're funny."

"I do, but not the point. Get me a beer. American, in a bottle."

"American? Sure you don't mean margarita, José?"

"Cause I'm Latino? That why?"

The guy shrugged and crossed his arms. "Don't care what the hell you call yourself, José."

"José. I like that. I don't look like one of your hunting buddies, my name must be José. What do I call you? You're white, so maybe Hitler? Elvis? Justin Bieber?"

"Time for you to go, José. I ain't serving your ass anymore."

Manny threw his drink at the man, glass and all. A soft toss—the bartender caught it but got sloshed. When he looked up, dripping, Manny had his badge out.

"I want a beer, Hillbilly Elegy. You don't speak English?"

"You're a cop?"

"Federal marshal. Bout to impound your truck, too, if I feel like it. You got a truck? Of course you got a truck." He reached over the bar and took a Budweiser out of the ice cooler. "I'll pay for this later. Meantime, you learn to make a whiskey sour. Us Americans like them."

The men held eyes. For Manny, who dealt death and stared it down since he was a boy, the conflict seemed natural and invigorating. Men such as him didn't look away. Another moment and the bartender conceded, set the drink down, and fetched a rag to clean his face.

Manny went back to their table, feeling mean and twitchy.

Beck slid the computer around. "Two prisoners are scheduled to be released Thursday. One Friday. The last one caught my eye..."

The two prisoners on Thursday were both African Americans in their fifties and he dismissed them. The man being released on Friday was Hispanic. Named Fidel Arroyo.

"I recognize him," said Manny. "Fidel."

"How?"

"Not sure." He reclined in his chair and drank some

Budweiser. His beer palate had improved under the August household's strict standards, and he judged it average at best. He drank more, determined to enjoy the classic American staple. He said, "Fidel Arroyo. Name doesn't ring a bell, but the face..."

Beck brought up Fidel's file. He was a powerful looking man. Strong neck, thick black hair. Stark cheekbones. "He's a handsome guy. He's in for breaking and entering, and assault. Plead guilty to get his sentence reduced. Out on good behavior six months early."

"Fidel Arroyo. That's not his name. I know this man." He closed his eyes and tilted his head back, searching memory banks.

"Someone you locked up, maybe?"

He didn't respond. It was possible.

She continued reading, "He was arrested in Washington D.C. No family, no history. Suspected stolen social security number. Maybe—"

Manny quit listening. The prisoner wasn't from Washington. That face didn't belong there. From L.A., maybe, his old life? Strange, Manny couldn't remember the man's voice. Just the face. Almost like he knew the guy, but they never met...

Manny's eyes snapped open. He sat up. "He's from California. That's where I knew him. Los Angeles."

"Who is he?"

"He is the reason El Gato is in America." He drank from the bottle. Set it down with a solid thunk. "His real name is Rafael García. He's Catalina's older brother."

20

Manny had a plan.

Beck listened to it and declared, "That's the worst, most outrageous thing I've ever heard."

"You say that a lot, Beck." Manny paced, fists on hips. "But fortune favors the brave."

"The bold."

"Whatever, shut up. Rafael gets out Friday. Tomorrow is Wednesday. We need action. Also, sorry for saying shut up."

She sat in the corner of the room, computer in her lap. She'd prefer to sit on the comfortable bed, but with another man in the room? With Manuel Martinez fuming mere feet from her? Absolutely not. Professional government agent or not, her mother would have a heart attack.

But, she supposed, this was superior to the previous night's work station—cramped in her car and hoping her partner hadn't been killed. On Monday she'd been securing servers and updating encryption technology on company phones, pleased with her career and not discontent with her personal life. Now she sat on thin carpet she was positive hadn't been recently vacuumed, in a small town hours from her apartment, working with a man whose modus operandi bordered on reckless to put it mildly, chasing a dangerous fugitive on a mission the FBI and NSA would disavow, entirely alone...

Plus, she was hungry. It was ten o'clock and they'd skipped dinner. Hungry and frustrated.

"This won't work," she said.

"Why not?"

"Because Rafael will recognize you. You were dating his sister."

"Rafael and I never met. We only occupied the same room a couple times. And I kept my head shaved then."

On screen she had prisoner transfer paperwork displayed. It would take her an hour, and constitute a felony. Much depended on the strength of their Supremacy License.

She said, "Special Agent Weaver won't approve of you going undercover inside a level five state prison. Rafael shouldn't even be there, considering his sentencing. Another option, we can hold his release and interrogate him."

"Rafael got picked up over a year ago, only the police didn't realize who they had. They charged his alias Fidel Arroyo with minor crimes unaware they should be prosecuting Rafael García for major. That's why he pled guilty —to keep his alias intact and get out of jail quickly. So Catalina bided her time, waiting for Fidel Arroyo to be released. If we delay his release she'll realize we know that Fidel is really Rafael, her brother. She'll vanish."

"She will anyway."

"Not till Saturday. This is still a game to her. She knows we don't want a national incident. There's a reason we don't have the Palace surrounded with two hundred officers, *sí*? If we hold her brother hostage, it escalates. That is what JFIC is for, arresting high-profile fugitives covertly without the government having to get its hands dirty."

"We need more help. Going undercover inside a state prison is a significant operation."

Manny didn't hear her. "She's hiding something, Beck. She's a danger, like a petulant child, and rattling entire countries is her toy. I never should have let her get on that plane."

A crease formed between her eyes, watching him pace. "What plane?"

"Ten years ago. She wasn't El Gato, she was a scared girl. She left and Central America was hard on her and she's broken now. Unstable. I could've made her stay. I could have demanded or begged or... She used to be about family and loyalty, and now most of her family's dead and she wants more power and she laughs about destroying economies. She's a killer and I could've stopped it."

Beck shifted on the floor to stretch her back and return circulation to her feet. "You're not responsible for El Gato's crimes."

Manny waffled his hand. "Debatable. I'm not letting her get away again. If I make contact with Rafael, maybe he'll talk."

"If it doesn't work, we can still apprehend El Gato at the airport, I suppose."

"She's not going to the airport," said Manny.

"You know?"

"I'm guessing."

"Then why would the Palace reserve a private plane on Saturday, the day after her brother's release?"

He waved her question away, irritated. "To throw us off track. She knows we're monitoring her."

"The jet at Roanoke Airport's a ruse? It was reserved through hidden back channels."

"I don't know, Beck. I'm thinking out loud and pretending to see things clearly. But it's possible."

Her computer beeped. She scanned the result. "Got a hit. Rafael García was mentioned in a note between the CIA and the Brazilian Intelligence Agency. Brazil held him briefly, two years ago, on suspicion of conspiracy during the election."

Manny crouched beside her to peer at the screen. She pretended she couldn't smell his cologne. He said, "Catalina mentioned Brazil's election. Using Honduran banana crops to swing votes, or something like that."

"That country is a wreck. Ready to collapse."

"I spent time there when I was young. The García family makes their money disrupting elections, seems like."

"Your breath smells like Christmas."

"Wintergreen mints. Focus, Beck."

"I am. Take a step backwards."

Manny raised and nodded to himself. "Tomorrow, bright and early, we're banging on the prison warden's door. Flash our badge and license. I'll go undercover as a prisoner until they release Rafael Friday. I have forty-eight hours to gain his trust and find out where El Gato plans to go. Once I do, I'll contact you and you spring me."

"That *cannot* be the best plan."

"Based on what I find, we'll alert Weaver. Maybe he'll

lead us to Catalina. Maybe she'll come to the prison. Maybe I'll kill him in jail. Who knows."

"Don't be cavalier. We're not assassins."

"Don't be naive. That is precisely what we are, when required. Think about it—we're after international terrorists. Terrorism is punishable by death. So maybe Rafael needs to die. That's not cavalier, that's charcuterie."

"Charcuterie?"

"Means perfect. And delicious."

She eyed him doubtfully. "I believe the correct definition is more—"

"Focus, Beck. We have a fugitive to catch."

Her phone rang, startling them both. Beck's eyebrow arched. "Weaver."

Anger flared in Manny's heart. In heaven there'd be no supervisors.

She put the phone on speaker and set it on the floor between them. "We're here, Special Agent."

"A situation has arisen," Weaver said, sounding hollow and tinny. "A half dozen deputy marshals are gathering in Harlan, Kentucky. They have a warrant and plan on storming the Palace at midnight."

"Storming the Palace with a half dozen?" Manny snorted. "That's it?"

Beck said, "They'll be killed."

"I just got off the phone with the Marshal in Louisville. He told me to jump back up the FBI asshole I crawled out of. Good ol' boy has stars in his eyes, thinking he'll catch El Gato. I don't know how he heard. I'm trying to get the Governor involved but it's slow going."

Manny glanced at his watch. Two hours from now. With a growl, he said, "They're going to get killed, and suddenly this is a national incident and Catalina will vanish."

"My thoughts exactly."

Manny took the pistols from his mattress and shoved them into his holsters. Grabbed his jacket. "I'm on the way. I'll get there in an hour."

"Dressed like *that?*"

He glanced down. He still wore the formal clothes for Catalina's dinner invitation. "I'm about to save the lives of six deputy marshals. It's important to look good doing it, right?"

"I'll get my stuff."

"No." He flung open the door, nearly hitting her. "Stay here. Get started on the prison paperwork, that's more important. I'll be back around one in the morning."

The door slammed after him.

Beck hit her fist against the carpet. What an infuriating pain in her neck. He'd be long gone, even if she tried to keep up. Her career had been running so smoothly— soon she'd be promoted out of Installation, assigned to Cryptanalysis and Exploitation. Her dream, back to headquarters. Except Manuel Martinez was going to get her demoted to sanitation.

For the phone's benefit, she said, "Sinatra is heading to Harlan. Text him directly."

"I will." The line went quiet, other than Weaver's keyboard clicking. After a long pause, "Sinatra's impetuous, isn't he. An asset and a liability."

Beck nodded to herself. "Special Agent, does one of us outrank the other?"

"Good question."

21

Gate City, Virginia to Harlan, Kentucky is sixty miles through curving country roads. Manny did it in forty-five minutes.

Harlan is small, nestled along the junction of Clover Fork and Martin's Fork rivers, pinned in by mountains. A likable place, thought Manny, as he flew up 421. It held old world charm, reminiscent of the towns in black and white television shows he'd seen, like Andy Griffith and something about a Beaver. Late at night, the lamp posts were lit and the downtown looked like an oil painting.

Noelle Beck called him. "The Louisville Marshal went dark. Weaver said she'll get him fired when this is done. I spoke with the Governor and he put me in touch with Harlan's mayor, who owns the local funeral home. He rang enough phones to discover the Sports Cafe on Eversole Street has its lights on, but the doors are locked and there are official cars parked outside. That's where the deputies are gathering, I bet, before heading to Pine Mountain."

"How much intel do they have about the Appalachian Palace?"

"Not much, evidently, otherwise they wouldn't try."

Manny glanced at his phone. Beck pushed through the address of the Sports Cafe. He said, "They know who El Gato is?"

"She's on a few most wanted lists, technically. The FBI must have a security leak. Somehow our surveillance of El Gato pinged in Louisville. With enough time, JFIC could back the marshal's office down but these are boys out in the country, playing cops and robbers and they aren't listening."

Manny turned onto Eversole Street. His headlights shot through narrow corridors of the downtown and high-lighted a man at the intersection.

He slammed his brakes, squealing. "Oh hell."

"What?"

Manny shoved open his door and got out. The town felt empty but clean, like they were on a movie set. The man on the corner was a handsome man in his sixties. He wore a flat cap and trench coat, despite the evening's warmth. His belt was white.

Manny said, "Hubert?"

Hubert, the Appalachian Palace's steward and manager, peered at him a moment. He smiled then without humor. "Ah, Mr. Martinez. I'm very sorry to see you here."

Manny read it all in Hubert's face. The man knew. He knew about the deputies gathering to knock on his door with plans to arrest his guest, and he'd come preemptively with one goal—execute them. His hit squad would be efficient and thorough and then they'd vanish.

Manny protected the realm.

Hubert protected his guests.

"Is Catalina here?"

"She is not. Although," Hubert said with a touch to his cap. "The same could be said about me."

"Call off your squad. I'll talk sense into the marshals. I'll send them home, guaranteed."

Hubert pulled the sleeve of his coat back to glance at his watch. "Festivities are about to begin. Too late, I'm afraid."

"No it's not, call them."

"I wish you hadn't come, Mr. Martinez."

"Because, *señor*, I'm a witness. I know you killed the deputies, I can identify you, and I know where you live."

The steward made a slight bow. "It's nothing personal, you understand. But...you just became a loose end."

Manny removed his Glock and waggled it. "Careful the things you say, Hubert."

Hubert smiled. "You won't shoot me. I'm unarmed."

"You might be surprised."

"I did my research. You're underworld material, Mr. Martinez. Brutal and tireless. Your hands are bloodier than most. In my line of work, you're worth two million a year. Yet you live by the same code all the fatally noble do. And you won't shoot me." He shrugged inside his trench coat. "You'd like it on my end, being a free agent. A lot more freedom."

Manny lowered his gun again, feeling foolish. The man called his bluff, and he wasted time talking. "Goodbye Hubert."

Hubert stepped off the curb and walked to a dark Lexus sedan on 1st Street. "I'm afraid so, Mr. Martinez. Best of luck."

Manny whipped off his sports jacket, threw it inside

the car, and yelled at the phone. "Beck, the Appalachian Palace security team is already here."

"Impossible. How did—"

"Call for ambulances."

Manny left the car door open and ran for the Sports Cafe. His shoes sounded like drums in the silence.

Idiots! This was such a stereotypical thing for deputy marshals to do. Meatheads, they were called. All muscle, no brain. Leap first, look later. Action junkies. Given a target, they chase it without a second thought. No regard for preparation or repercussion.

His kind of people.

How quickly things change. He'd raced here to warn them about the lion's den. But the lions got here first.

The Cafe was small and shining like a jack-o'-lantern in the dark. A half dozen cars were parked out front, crowding the thin street.

He couldn't see Hubert's men but he heard them spring their ambush, a sound he'd remember the rest of his days.

Assault rifles roared to life in the still and empty downtown. The noise echoed from everywhere, but he guessed Hubert's security team had used the back door of the Cafe, catching the deputies off guard.

He sprinted around the line of cars. Front door coming in range, his heart hammering.

Two of Hubert's men were waiting in the shadows near the entrance. If the deputies tried to run out the front door they'd be cut down. So focused were they on their assignment that they didn't hear him coming.

The sound of gunfire inside the Cafe nauseating Sinatra. He felt like vomiting. He was too late to save the deputies inside. But he could avenge them.

"Turn around, amigos!" he shouted, startling them. A foolish notion; he wouldn't shoot men in the back.

The two men crouching in the shadows twisted. One of them Manny recognized—Nicholás the sentry, the man who'd clubbed him in the back. Both ambushers held assault rifles.

Time shifted into a slower gear. Manny didn't break stride. He leveled the Glock, his right arm straight, left crooked at the elbow. Years of training painted a terminus on his target, his hands and eyes working in concert with his balance and speed. Like a laser sight only he could see. Small adjustments steadied the bouncing terminus...

He squeezed.

The weapon blasted its load and Nicolás's head caved between the eyes. The other man flinching sideways, trying to aim. Manny shot him quick—a lucky strike, fatal, near the hairline. He reached their bodies and fired twice more each, the rounds to the chest. Six total he'd fired. He ejected his magazine, pocketed it, and rammed in another.

Errant rounds inside the Cafe perforated the glass storefront. Bullets thudding into parked cars.

The wide pane to the right of the door shattered, falling in wedges and splinters. A tremendous crash, though not as loud as the assault rifle chatter.

A man staggering through the door and onto the sidewalk.

Even in the dim light, Manny identified a marshal—beefy, wearing a ballistic vest, tattoos on his arms. He caught another round in the back, absorbed by the plate.

Manny gathered a two-step running start, caught the man with his shoulder, and barreled him out of harm's way. More bullets raining into the car doors. Manny landed on top of the man and rolled off, his Glock snapping up to cover the door.

Inside the gunfire ceased.

He was too late, he knew. Hubert brought professionals. Everyone inside was dead by now. His stomach churned, sick with adrenalin and fear.

He held the pistol in his right fist. With his other hand he groped for the deputy. "Hey, *hombre*, get up. We need to go." His voice sounded calm.

Across the street from the Cafe was an old television station, now vacant. One story. Had Manny been looking, he'd have seen a hostile rise on the roof, brandishing one of the launchers from the Appalachian Palace. He'd be impressed to discover it was a military-grade Mk 153 shoulder-launcher, housing a thermobaric rocket. Perfect for obliterating evidence.

But Manny wasn't looking. Ignorant of the danger, he took hold of the deputy's vest and dragged him to the curb.

The man on the roof waited, pausing for his colleagues to clear, and fired.

The rocket jumped into the Cafe and erupted. Fire and light and noise. The detonation created overpressure inside the building, an effect which shattered the air and breathed violently inward. Had Manny been fifteen feet closer, his eyes and ears and lungs would've been destroyed, possibly sucked out of his body.

The Cafe broke and collapsed. Propane tanks burst and ignited; shrapnel and gaseous flames flung wide. The fiery wave rolled outwards, then rose into the dark sky.

For a handful of heartbeats, Manny thought he'd died. Couldn't see, couldn't hear, like he'd been spun out of a blender. His shirt was on fire. He screwed up his eyes and pressed against his ears. Everything hurt. His senses sputtered and came back online.

The deputy marshal groaned again and crawled behind a car and collapsed.

"Get *under* the car," called Manny in a hoarse voice. "And stay there."

He had to go. Immediately.

They'd be coming for him now.

22

Manny's car still idled at the intersection of Eversole and Main. He limped into sight as one of Hubert's extermination crew ran for the Camaro's open car door. If they stole his car, he'd be trapped with the lions.

He paused. Assumed a Weaver firing stance. His hands shook. Shirt smoldering. He glared down the Glock's sight and tracked the man. Held his breath and squeezed.

The Glock kicked and the man's shoulder spit blood. The impact spun him around. Manny fired again and missed, his target scrambling behind the line of cars.

Two rounds fired. Seven left.

The night was warming with noise. Sirens and dogs barking.

Manny ran for his Camaro, firing wildly at the man he'd shot.

"Stay down!" he shouted.

He reached his car—it was open and idling; a careless and fortunate mistake on his part. He dropped into gear, and his eyes widened—to his left, standing on the second floor of the old bank and silhouetted by the night's perfectly full moon, a man hoisted a rocket launcher onto his shoulder and aimed.

"*Ay hala*," he grumbled.

He stomped the gas. The car responded beautifully, surging forward fast enough to take his breath. He needed all 650 horsepower.

Eyes on his rearview, he turned right into W..l Flavor, wheels screaming, and the man with the launcher fired. Rockets travel too fast for any real evasive maneuver, but it was unguided—Manny swerved to the left and the printing shop on the corner detonated with the errant missile.

Manny executed a hard left going fifty miles per hour. He jerked the steering wheel, downshifted to break traction and spin the tires, and turned into the skid. The Camaro fishtailed without losing speed, gripped the road again heading south on 421, and shot forward.

He touched the shifter and reached ninety, jetting from downtown. Headlights flared behind.

Of course he'd be pursued. Hubert would be up to his ears in cops if Manny escaped.

Chances were, the car was a black Toyota sedan. Camry or Avalon. Maybe Lexus. He'd seen a fleet of them at the Appalachian Palace. Probably only a 3.5L V6, a toy compared to his American muscle. But on these twisting roads through the mountainous countryside the smaller car could compete if expertly driven, relaying Manny's location to other cars.

He shifted and eased off the gas, arcing through a curve. Bringing them closer. His Camaro pulsed restlessly, reminding him of resources yet untapped.

The pursuing sedan converged and flicked its high

beams, blinding him. Manny buzzed down his window—
night air rushed in like a hurricane.

A pop behind. Pistol shot. Missed.

From inside his pocket, Manny detected a vibration.
An incoming call but his phone was inaccessible. He activated the car's Bluetooth and sudden ringing filled the
interior. He pressed a button on the steering wheel to
answer.

"Sinatra! Where are—"

"Listen, Beck. I'm heading south on 421. Hubert and
the Appalachian guys massacred the marshals. If I don't
return, you'll find my wrecked car a mile or two out of
Harlan."

"Did you—"

"I'll call you back."

He punched the button again, hanging up.

Another pop from the Toyota and a bullet punctured
Manny's rear windshield. From the sound of it, the bullet
lodged inside the passenger seat back. Small shards of
glass sprinkled his dash. Through the rearview, he glared
out the jagged hole.

"Bastards. *Cabrón!*"

The Camaro crested a rise and entered a quarter-mile
straightaway. He pushed another button and the vehicle's
'hands free' guidance activated. Sensors would make
small adjustments to keep his car within the lines.

He unbuckled his safety belt, twisted enough to get his
left knee onto the seat, and pushed halfway out of the
window, facing backwards. Left hand bracing inside, right
hand gripping the Glock and training on the bouncing
Toyota. The wind tore at his hair and ruined shirt.

He fired twice. His rounds sparked against the
pursuing windshield, inflicting no damage.

Both the driver and passenger of the Toyota returned fire. Careless shots, only sticking their pistol out.

Manny returned to his seat and resumed control. Fastened his belt again.

Bullet-proof glass. Made things trickier.

Five rounds remaining in the magazine.

They went around a sweeping curve in close formation, like Blue Angels. A road sign proclaimed they'd entered Chevrolet, Kentucky. The symbolism pleased him. To his right, the moon reflected off a river.

Highway 421 elevated from the earth, becoming a bridge to span the railroad and Martin's Fork river. The bridge ran for half a mile and Manny floored the gas pedal. The Camaro leaped ahead and the speedometer eased beyond a hundred and thirty-five.

The Toyota accelerated but had no ability to match top speeds.

At the far end of the bridge Manny went airborne before dropping onto the ramp. Elegantly the shocks cushioned his impact. He killed his lights, plunging into darkness. Braked hard, tires screaming down to the fifties, and then yanked the hand brake. His rear wheels locked and he cut to the left. He shot into the other lane and the rear of the car fishtailed behind. He spun into the skid, revved the RPMs, released the hand brake, and straightened, now heading back the way he came. A slick move he learned training with the California Highway Patrol.

The Toyota saw none of it, hidden by the bridge's brow. They hit the ramp going ninety and failed to notice Manny's dark car at the base in the oncoming lane.

He was ready. As the Toyota neared and passed, he fired five times at the driver side tire. Sparks flew and synthetic rubber surrendered in three places, going flat in an instant. The sedan lost control. The driver overcorrected and shot into the trees bordering the highway. A stout pine arrested their advance, demolishing the engine and inflating airbags.

Ejected the empty clip. Slammed in another.

Manny turned south, firing twice at the sedan to keep them inside, before opening the throttle. Half a mile away, he turned on his headlights again and took a detour.

He'd have done so with a smug smile if his face didn't ache from the night's festivities.

23

Manny called Beck. She answered before the first ring.

"I'm monitoring the position of your phone. Appears you survived," she said.

"Never in doubt."

"Are you wounded?"

"Yes," he said.

"Where?"

"All of it."

"Harlan neighborhoods placed over a hundred 911 calls so far. Weaver wants a report."

"Hubert killed them. I took out a couple of his team, might've saved one deputy."

Beck asked, "Did Hubert see you?"

"Yes. We spoke."

"Darn it."

"Sometimes, Beck, you need to curse. It helps."

"The FBI will get involved now. En masse. Six federal officers were assaulted, a national incident, and they won't sit quietly."

"Right."

"And we're obligated to report Hubert being on site."

"Which means the feds will descend on the Palace. JFIC will deactivate and pretend we were never involved."

Meaning, his job was done.

She said, "Silver lining. The FBI's wanted to knock on their door for years. Getting a warrant and the manpower should be easy, after our report. And APOG is too smart to resist now."

Manny sighed and rubbed at his eyes, which hurt. "They won't find anything. Even now, Hubert will order a clean house. Shifting everything offsite. Catalina is likely already moving to a secondary location."

"Who knows where that'll be."

He nodded to himself. "I lost her."

MANNY FOUND AN ALL-NIGHT convenience store near Stone Mountain Park and eased to a stop in the back. The Camaro powered down, pleased to have been put to good use. He'd taken back roads for the past hour, ensuring Hubert's hit squad couldn't find him.

He sat in the car, seething. It'd all gone wrong. Somehow the thing had slipped out of his control. He banged his fist against the wheel.

Damn it! He had the assignment for five minutes and blew it. The job of his dreams. They came to him specifically and he didn't get it done. He glared at his phone and the messages from Beck he hadn't answer yet.

>> Got off the phone with Weaver. She's pleased. You identified Hubert and one of the deputies is alive. Thanks to us, the FBI will have a warrant for the Appalachian Palace within eight hours.

>> She agrees, El Gato has flown the coup. Plan is to arrest her at the airport on Saturday. She wants you there.

>> In the meantime, we return to normal duty tomorrow morning.

What a waste. Instead of being in the field alone, he'd be working with an enormous joint task force to storm the Palace—they'd find nothing.

That's what galled him. Marshals being killed and then chasing dead ends. And the FBI, one of the finest agencies on planet earth, being leg around by the nose. Hubert and the others were two steps ahead, and Catalina was gone, and *still* the feds would go through the motions. Wasting their time. And his.

Yes sir.

Yes ma'am.

Whatever you say, sir.

Get on the plane, ma'am. Fly to Honduras. I won't object.

He got out and mournfully inspected the bullet wounds. Two in the bumper, plus the busted rear windshield. He patted the Camaro—she deserved better.

A bell rang as he pushed into the store. The lone clerk restocking bags of potato chip did a double take. He grabbed a tube of Neosporin and some burn cream and went into the bathroom.

Yikes. He looked rough. Still swollen and bruised from his fight with Julio, now he bore second degree burns. Some of his eyebrow had singed. He cleaned himself with cold water and a paper towel. Rubbed aloe on the burns and Neosporin on the cuts. Came out and grabbed a bottle of Tylenol.

The clerk came to ring him. Young guy, late twenties, fat, curly hair. "You in a movie?"

Manny asked, "What?"

"You're a movie star, right? Is there a movie shoot nearby?"

He shook his head. "No stunts. Just a weird night." He gave him the Tylenol and the boxes he'd opened.

"You from Kentucky? Hear about the shooting? Gonna be big news."

"I bet."

"Anything else? Something to drink?"

"No. Well..." Manny turned. "Something with caffeine."

"Coffee? Coke?"

Coffee sounded good. But his feet took him to the refrigerators. To the Coca-Cola. He found a glass bottle and took it out, enjoying the cold surface.

Catalina said the American recipe tasted better than the Honduran. That day in Compton, she'd been drinking one. Ten years ago. The day he was supposed to meet Rafael.

He twisted the top, a fizzy hiss, and drank some.

Awful. Like sucking sour syrup. The pure sugar might arrest his whole system. What was Catalina thinking?

She was gone from the Palace by now. She wouldn't take the chance. She was in a car, traveling to another safe house, probably glaring out the window.

But...her brother wasn't going anywhere. He'd lost *her*, but not *him*.

Manny paid and returned to his Camaro. He opened his phone's calendar and looked at his upcoming work schedule. As he thought; Thursday—witness protection paperwork; Friday—prisoner transport. Boring work. And they'd be delayed for the fruitless raid on the Appalachian Palace. But the tasks waited when he returned...

He liked his job. He hunted dangerous men for a living. And women. Pursuit and peril in service to his country. But the days of adventure mingled with hours of boredom and drudgery and prisoner transport and paperwork. How long could he fake it? Being a gentleman didn't mean he was professional—he didn't care about advancement or accolades.

Catalina. Drinking the Coke. Begging him to get on the plane. *You are more*, she said.

He wasn't more. But he was something the other deputies weren't. His anger penetrated several layers lower. He hadn't survived hell and come out meek. Was the sophisticated American gentleman role he played fake? No, but it was only half of him. The other half of him, like his car, grew restless.

He caught criminals for a living. And he was good at it. Get on the plane, Manny. You are more.

Not every opportunity touched down in Honduras.

Some of them landed him in prison. And at the moment, that's exactly where he wanted to be.

He punched a message to Beck.

You're really good at this.

But I gotta do something. Alone.

Back in a few days.

He turned off his phone so she couldn't track it, buying him time and possibly saving her job. He started the car and poured out the Coke. Catalina wouldn't get away so easily again.

24

Warden Brooks wasn't having it. And he wasn't pleased at the mere request this early. The breakfast sandwiches his wife'd packed him sat unopened in their Saran Wrap cocoons, next to the Stanley Classic. He'd never been military and he didn't strike Manny as police, though he must have the background somewhere. The two diplomas on the wall declared degrees in fancy script Manny couldn't decipher. Brooks wore authority like a factory manager— intelligent and efficient, not mean. Shorter than Manny with thick curly hair.

"Like hell," said Warden Brooks.

"You have no choice." As an afterthought, then, to grease the wheels, "Sir."

"My prison, my choice. And you're not going in. Not without a direct phone call from Virginia's attorney general."

Manny flashed his credentials again, like a poker player. "Trust me, Mr. Brooks."

The warden's desk was bolted to the floor, empty of sharp or hard objects. The office's guest chair was also bolted down. Steep green mountains were visible through the security window to the northwest.

"On earth happened to you, anyway?" He indicated Manny's charred outfit and fresh wounds.

"Long night."

"Involved in that godawful marshal massacre in Kentucky?"

Manny said again, "Long night."

Warden Brooks plucked Manny's proffered laminated card and dropped it on his desk without looking. He picked up the phone and said, "Call for Allan, please. My office."

Radios squawked and Allan appeared soon after. A giant of a man, with a goatee and shaved head. Eyes like coal drills.

"Marshal, this is Allan Johnston, our deputy warden and chief of security. Allan, this idiot wants to go undercover as a prisoner for two days."

Allan Johnston looked too tough to express surprise.

Manny said, "Name's Sinatra. Deputy marshal. Professional idiot. Check my credentials. I bet whoever gets you as Secret Santa comes away disappointed."

Johnston remained quiet. He held an iPad.

The warden said, "Marshal, you ain't spent much time in a prison, I take it."

"I spent a *lot* of time in them, señor. On both sides of the bars."

"Then you know it is a world unto itself. The prison's residents have their own ecosystem and atmosphere and *code* of conduct that even the security staff can't entirely see. It is a violent and cruel world. And sometimes my staff is worse than the inmates. I don't have the manpower nor the time nor the inclination to babysit you."

"Never had a babysitter in my life. Not even as a kid when my mother took off for benders."

Allan Johnston the deputy warden rumbled, "They find out you're police, they'll kill you."

"It'll take all of them."

"I think you might be an asshole, Mr. Sinatra. An idiot and an asshole." Warden Brooks slid the card off his desk and inspected it. He appeared underwhelmed. Weird, because Manny thought it was a good photo of him. "Make matters worse, I leave first light for Disney World. My family's first vacation in two years and I'm not missing it. My daughter's only been asking for months and my wife threatened to leave me if I don't take her out of this hellhole now and then, and here you are."

"I need a room near Fidel Arroyo. I need to keep my phone under my pillow. I need my schedule synched with his. And I need out Friday afternoon."

Warden Brooks scoffed. "A *room?*"

Johnston's eyes narrowed. "Arroyo? Why Arroyo?"

A buzzing came over the loud speakers. Somewhere within the prison, directions echoed off painted cinderblock. The floor shook with hydraulic doors slamming open.

Warden Brooks waved toward the deputy warden. "Allan Johnston is a good man. He's in charge while I'm gone. But he's not here all day. You understand that?" He lowered into his chair with a squeak. Examined the card and punched things into his computer.

Johnston asked again, "Why Arroyo?"

"I need information out of him."

"What kind?"

"Top secret kind."

"What office are you with?"

"Roanoke Marshal's Office"

Johnston said, "This is not a good idea, you going in."

"Only one I got right now."

The deputy warden crossed his arms. "You know Collin Parks out of Roanoke?"

"Sure. Short. Cauliflower ears. Guy's a wimp. Sometimes I daydream about kicking his ass."

"Collin's my cousin."

"Oof. Sorry to hear that."

Warden Brooks had gone very quiet at the computer. His face lost some color. Without taking his eyes off the screen, he said, "The hell kinda credentials you got?"

Johnston asked, "What do you mean?"

"Look at this." Brooks swiveled the monitor toward Johnston, who came around the desk for a better view.

He read and whistled. "That's the damnedest."

Manny grinned. Supremacy License still in place. "I'm a huge deal. I'm like Ronald Reagan, my importance cannot be overstated."

"Well, Ronald, this says I give you any trouble, I can expect to be visited by the Director of the FBI, the Attorney General, the Governor, and potentially arrested under Article VI, Section 2 of the constitution."

Chances were, that wouldn't happen. Though he retained the license a few more days, Beck's preliminary report to Weaver would indicate no threats to national security.

In fact he'd probably be fired soon, for insubordination.

None of these thoughts he offered out loud.

Johnston asked, "And you're doing this alone."

"Yep. Small operation. Only need one guy."

"Well, damn it, your funeral, I reckon." The warden

pressed a button and his clerical assistant came in. He told her, "Photocopy the credentials please, and get the waivers. You're gonna sign your life away, same as the others, Sinatra. We get reporters occasionally, wanna spend the night for the experience. For the *enrichment*. Scared straight programs, that kind of thing. But those are closely supervised. You on the other hand—"

"If I'm supervised, they'll see. Gotta be authentic."

Johnston nodded, running his finger across his iPad. "Best the guards don't know either."

"Where's Arroyo housed?"

"Looking." A pause. "B-212. Nothing open near him."

"Hear that...Sinatra?" said the warden, with a quick glance at the computer screen to confirm the codename. "No rooms near him and I'm not shuffling inmates. Not that it matters anyway, not like you two could pass notes. What's Arroyo's job?"

"Kitchen. He's there now."

"Here's what I'll do, Sinatra. Give you a cell in Cell Block B. Put you in the kitchen with him. Give you the same dining hall schedule. And it's up to you to find him in the yard. I get back, I'll attend your funeral."

Manny nodded. Better than he hoped for.

Johnston asked, "How'll I know when you want to be released?"

Manny reached into his pocket for his phone. Waggled it. "I'll call you. Phone will be in my pillowcase."

"I put you in. Then I forget about you until I get your call. That sound right?"

"Right."

"Great singer, Sinatra. Liked that guy."

Manny jerked a thumb at himself. "Heroes, both of us."

25

Manny marched the sidewalk through the North Yard. Deputy Warden Johnston walked on his right, and detention officer Norris on his left. His wrists were cuffed and he wore a bright yellow jumpsuit, meant to make inmates conspicuous if they escaped. Fortunately, he thought, he had the skin tone to wear it well.

Wallens Ridge State Prison felt alien, a remote planet of concrete and metal. Encircled by double layers of security fencing with razor wire. Most of the 'yard' was asphalt. Two armed guards patrolled the roof of each cell block and the central structures.

The entirety of earth can be divided into two realms —inside a prison and everywhere else. Inside a prison is not America, it's *other*, it's foreign. It's hard to move between the two realms and Manny felt the first door acutely as it slammed behind. They walked alone. Inmates weren't playing ball or lounging outside this early.

Norris looked country. A thin guy but built with wiry strength. His short beard grew patchy and his eyes were different colors, one blue and one green. He asked, "Says inmate Sinatra's already been through orientation?"

"More or less." Deputy Warden Allan Johnston's mouth was turned down, eyes hard. They spoke quietly.

"And I'm the only officer who knows?"

"That's right. No one else finds out."

"What if something happens?"

"Treat him like a normal prisoner. He breaks the rules, move him to solitary. He's being threatened, ring the multidisciplinary team."

Detention officer Norris asked, "But what if it's a *bad* something?"

"Bad enough, come get me," said Johnston.

"What if you ain't here, sir?"

Manny, though possessing nerves of steel and a heart that pumped red, white, and blue, quietly wished the prison staff would quit vocalizing the very real possibility something *bad* was going to happen.

"Bad enough, get him out. He dies, wake me at home. Other than that, he's a regular inmate until he calls," said Johnston.

Norris lowered the iPad he'd been scanning and he grabbed Manny's elbow. They stopped near the entrance to Cell Block B. It loomed like a monstrous tombstone. Norris indicated it with his chin. "That's my cell block. I'm the superintendent. Get it? And even I don't know everything what goes on. You get it, Sinatra?"

"I get it, Norris."

"You know the convict code? The subset of rules the inmates live by? It's their code. The gist of it, it's inmates against correctional officers. Them versus us. They live and die by it. You know what happens they find out who you are?"

"I know."

"Do you? Cause they won't kill you. Not immediately. Most likely, I won't know about it for hours. And when I do, might take a while to locate you. At least parts of you. Get it, Sinatra?"

Manny nodded. Cleared his throat. "Sounds like a tight ship you run."

"It's prison. You don't like it, turn around." Norris pointed at Manny's face. "You need medical attention? Looks fresh. Got burn marks on the back of your neck, too."

"You should see the other guy."

Norris said, "Gawd almighty, this is nuts, sir."

"Got that right." At the door to Cell Block B, Allan Johnston stopped. Said, "I'll have my phone on, Sinatra. You're on your own until you call." A final nod and he marched back the way he came.

Norris picked up another detention officer and they led Manny through two sets of heavy doors with small security windows. Inside, inmates mopped the floors. Cleaned the bathrooms. Performed duties which earned them as much as four dollars a day. Guards stood at all points of egress and along the walkways—they carried mace and tasers, no firearms. Loud voices banged hard off the painted cinderblock walls. Doors were blue, walls white.

They led him to the third floor to B-305. Norris spoke into a radio on his shoulder and the door unlocked. The man inside, Manny's cell mate, rolled off his bunk and backed to the wall out of habit.

"Ignacio, meet your new life partner," said Norris in an unnaturally hard voice. Ignacio stayed at the wall, didn't reply. "This here's..." Norris checked his iPad. "...Sinatra.

Ain't that a riot, Ignacio? Sinatra, this here's your new home."

The PA system blared to life, instructing inmates inside Cell Block B onto their bunks. Doors rammed open. Manny knew the drill—the prison physically counted inmates four times a day. This was likely the second.

Norris gave Manny a shove.

"Nine o'clock count. Get on your bunk and stay there, Sinatra. And welcome to the Rock."

Ignacio, a heavier Hispanic man, maybe sixty, swollen dark eyes, lowered himself back to the bottom bunk with a grunt. Manny hopped onto the top. Slid out his cell phone and shoved it into his pillow case.

He stuck his head over the side.

"*Habla Inglés?*"

"*Sí,*" said Ignacio.

"The white guard, Norris. He called this place the Rock."

"Nickname. For our cell block. What happened to your face?"

Manny slipped into Spanish. "They transferred me from Red Onion. My cell mate, he went through my things, messed with my bed, so in the kitchen I burned him with a propane tank and match. I got burned too. My lawyer moved me here until the trial."

Ignacio looked as though he had questions but remained quiet. Manny's message was delivered—don't mess with my stuff. Especially the pillow case.

Two guards walked past, performing the count. They stopped at B-305, had a discussion about the new guy, and went on.

Manny leaned forward, ready to be taken to the kitchen. To Rafael.

26

No one came for inmate Sinatra.

He waited an hour before walking to the rail and scanning the cell block's interior. Half the inmates were resting in their bunk, half were busy working. A couple of the guards eyed him but said nothing.

While he leaned against the rail, debating whether or not to find a guard and explain he was new and needed to report to the kitchen, Bill Wolfe strolled through the common area of the cell block, three levels below. Bill was a white supremacist and possessed the tattoos on his scalp to prove it. Wolfe had alopecia—no body hair. None. He'd gotten more muscular since Manny'd seen him last, eighteen months ago, when Manny ran the man's Harley Davidson off Route 11 in Pulaski, Virginia, and found ten pounds of crystal meth in his possession. Bill Wolfe was a repeat offender—he ran crank and had been wanted for assaulting a minor, for hate crimes, skipping court dates, child support, and a slew of other things Manny couldn't remember.

Here he was, directly below, serving thirty years

because Manny brought him in with a broken arm, an orbital fracture, and severe burns on his legs.

Two other hulking white men with shaved heads mingled with Wolfe until guards shouted to disperse them. Wolfe's face twisted in a mocking smile and he returned to his mop, his gaze traveling upwards.

Manny swiveled away to his cell, keeping his face hidden. Better to remain unseen by Bill Wolfe. He hopped onto his bunk and laid on the scratchy gray wool blanket.

Ay! This was an unexpected hurdle. He needed to meet Rafael García without getting killed by prisoners he put here. Hopefully his injuries would be sufficient camouflage, otherwise they'd cut out his eyes and tongue with a shiv. He'd seen it happen.

Ignacio and a third of the inmates left before lunch for various jobs. Manny, bored and frustrated, rolled to his side and powered on his phone. The screen lit up with accumulated notifications.

Special Agent Weaver sent irate texts and a voice mail, which he deleted without listening to.

Marshal Warren also left a voicemail. Manny kept it for later.

Most texts were from Noelle Beck, angry and concerned.

Had the shootout in Harlan happened only twelve hours ago? Felt like a month.

He scanned the texts again. The marshals wanted to question him about the massacre in Kentucky; the FBI needed his input on the Appalachian Palace; Weaver demanded a final report on El Gato; and who knew what Marshal Warren wanted.

So. Much. Bureaucracy.

So. Many. Meetings.

And too much paperwork.

Didn't they see? Didn't they realize this whole thing hinged on Catalina García and she was gone? *Los tontos y los idiotas!* Manny was the only one with a lead, was the only one sticking his neck out, and his squadron of bosses wanted reports.

He knew this stunt would most likely result in his termination. He cared not.

Well, he cared not much. They wanted a Yes Man, they should've asked someone else. Someone weaker.

He typed a message to Beck. Sent it. Copied it and sent it to Weaver too.

Chasing a lead on El Gato. Will surface again on Friday. Should have more intel then. Hasta luego.

Then he powered down his phone to conserve battery.

He stared at the ceiling, trying to remember if Ethan Hunt or James Bond ever got themselves purposefully thrown into prison.

27

Cell Block B, or the Rock, has lunch at 12:30pm.

The buzzer rang to begin the controlled mass movement. For the first time in his life, Manny wished he was shorter. Easier to blend in, walk unseen. He hunched his shoulders, head down, and moved with the mob of orange and yellow. He scanned everywhere—no Rafael.

Bill Wolfe fell in not ten steps ahead.

And to Manny's left, he spotted Chilly the Kid. Small-time muscle for hire out of Roanoke, worked with Marcus Morgan and Big Will, known for breaking teeth. Manny'd beaten him within an inch of his life.

He slowed, letting the hungry crowd surge past. He couldn't go to the chow hall and eat with the general population. Too many familiar faces. Faces that hated him.

One of the new guards saw him lingering. The guard who'd walked with Norris. He shouted, "Hey Sinatra, you going for food?"

"Think I'll skip it. Head to the yard for air. That cause you any problems?"

"Suit yourself."

Soon the Rock was empty. Manny wandered upstairs to the second floor and peered into B-212. Catalina's brother's room. No one home.

The cell of Rafael García was immaculate. The toilet/sink combo gleamed. The desktop was clean and the books in the shelves underneath neatly organized. Beds made with hospital corners.

Manny debated going in. The door stood wide open, after all. He knew he'd find nothing of value. But usually the best stuff was found where it shouldn't be. His fingers drummed on the door.

Ay dios mio, how quickly roles change. He was an officer of the law, hesitant to enter an empty cell. For fear of upsetting the inmates and prison guards.

"Hey. Sinatra." It was Norris, the only man in Cell Block B who knew the truth. He crossed his arms and watched. "You're an inmate. You gotta follow the rules."

Manny said, "Yeah, that's weird. Not used to it."

"You know who lives there?"

"One of them."

"The two men in B-212, they don't play. You don't sit in their seats. You don't look at them. You don't watch television if they already are. They walk into the bathroom, you step out. They sit at a table, you get up. And you don't look into their room."

Manny's fists reflexively balled. These were men he liked to chase. Serious gangsters with pride the size of Escalades. These were men he enjoyed collaring, hauling in before a judge. The bigger they are...

"You're in Wallens Ridge, now, Sinatra. Best learn the rules real fast," said Norris, full of meaning.

Manny nodded. Two days. He could play meek for two days. "Yes sir. Maybe I'll walk the yard."

"You do that, Sinatra. And stay out of the crowd. That's a mighty fine place to get butchered."

The guards didn't look at Manny as he went outside. A handful of inmates were in the yard—the smaller ones who didn't trust the chow hall. They jogged or did pull-ups on the bars. No one touched the basketball or went on the court. Little guys not allowed.

Manny walked the track, hands in his pockets, thinking over Rafael's reputation. In Los Angeles, Rafael hadn't been a renowned tough guy, not someone to personally enforce the rules. Most likely he was using his finances to buy muscle at Wallens Ridge—purchasing phone cards so guys could call their mommas, supplying the pot, getting favors with his influence over the black market. The man with the money makes the rules.

Lunch ended for Cell Block A and Cell Block B and the inmates flooded outdoors—each block had its own yard. Manny stayed near the fence, watching.

Rafael Garcia, or Fidel Arroyo, came out near the end. He walked with a coterie of five guys. His posse. They didn't speak and they remained with him until he began walking the track. With no words spoken, two of the guys walked by his side while the rest filtered away.

A hundred and fifty inmates were in the yard, Manny estimated. Twenty of them played basketball on the two courts, while others watched and shouted. The bigger guys worked on exercise bars. Quieter inmates watched the mountains, staying out of trouble.

Rafael came Manny's way with his security detail, both Latinos. Manny stepped off the track to let him pass.

He was still a handsome guy. Thick black hair, sharp cheekbones. He'd grown circles under his eyes since Manny'd seen him in Los Angeles and a new scar ran from his ear down his neck.

Manny watched him pass and waited. His pulse increased, being this close. Rafael kept walking, hands clasped behind his back. He alternated between looking at the path and watching clouds.

You get out in two days, Rafael. Where you going?

Rafael completed the circuit and started another. He was watched by inmates he passed, the way powerful men often were.

This time, thought Manny, we talk.

The group of three reached him and Manny said, "Arroyo. You remember me?"

The skin around the man's eyes tightened and he made a "Hm-um," noise. That was all, didn't break stride.

"Arroyo," said Manny again, now talking to his back.

One of his guards gave Manny a shove. "Hey, pretty little fishy. Hell you think you are?"

"I want to talk with—"

"Shame, that pretty face of yours gets shoved in the disposal, little fishy."

Well.

I didn't come here to play nice.

Manny took a step, fist balled at his side.

He said, "Maybe you and me—"

Behind them, sudden chaos. Sounded like a herd of howler monkeys throwing a parade. A man was dragged into the center of the basketball court, a big white guy. The mob descended on him, kicking and punching. The white guy tried to roll away, but he was surrounded by twenty. He was attacked by every ethnicity. His resistance didn't last long under the brutal assault.

Manny jogged toward the mob. Instincts kicking in—he had to stop it.

He got close and someone grabbed him by the arm. Ignacio, his cell mate.

"Stay here," the man said in Spanish.

"They'll kill him."

"Stay here. The man will live. Do not interfere with the code."

The noise and the beating intensified, mob mentality feeding on itself. Savage mankind without restraint.

The PA system erupted. A horn blaring. Guards ran into the yard with tasers and tear gas canisters ready.

Quick as a switchblade, the assault was over. The roaring and bloodthirsty crowd turned innocent and obedient in a snap. Men turned and milled into the dispersing crowd.

The guards put on gloves and picked up the bloody and broken body. His jumpsuit was torn, his face shattered. He could barely see or stand.

Without having to ask, Manny knew—there'd be no punishment for the attackers. Guards tended to trust the judgment of the group. If the community decided discipline was needed, often it was. And by siding with the group the guards maintained the delicate balance of order.

He asked, "A racial thing, you think?"

Ignacio shrugged. "Sometimes. Sometimes it's territory or property."

"What'll they do with him?"

"Put him in solitary a few days. Maybe a week or two."

Manny's eyes widened. "Punish the guy who got his ass beat?"

"He deserved it. And solitary keeps him safe. By the way. I see you talking with Arroyo," said Ignacio. He pressed his finger into Manny's chest. "Do it again and you are next. Trust me."

Manny skipped dinner that night. He had a job to do, which didn't involve fighting Bill Wolfe or Chilly the Kid or anyone else in here who might recognize him. One of the prison staff came by at seven, told him he'd be woken for kitchen duty tomorrow at 4:30am.

Ignacio took him to a locker and shared out of his stash of Ramen noodles. They waited in line to heat it in the microwave and then ate in their cell.

Manny Martinez, proud practitioner of a ketogenic lifestyle, hungrily devoured the entire bowl, carbs and all. He wiped his mouth and said, "*Que susto! Delicioso, gracias.*"

"That's the only one you get. Cost me half a day's work."

"When is light's out?"

"Gotta be in bunks at nine." Ignacio looked out of their cell at the large clock, near the ceiling. "Fifteen minutes."

Manny moved quickly down the raised walkway, overlooking the common area. Bill Wolfe and his gang of white supremacists played cards at the far table. No sign of Chilly. He jogged down the stairs and moved to B-212.

Next door to Rafael, a group had gathered to watch television. The early NBA game, Sixers versus Lakers. Rafael's cell was quiet.

Manny knocked on the open door.

Rafael, reading at the desk, tilted his head for a better view of the intruder.

The big man from earlier in the yard, Rafael's body guard, emerged from the cell and blocked Manny's view.

"Ugh, you again," said Manny. "What, the guy needs a babysitter?"

Manny's arms were grabbed from behind. The big man hit Manny in the stomach, a movement so quick and violent he had no time to brace. All the air left his lungs. Another punch came close to breaking his cheekbone.

The vice grip released.

Manny fell to his knees. That happened *so* fast. He tried to gasp but nothing came. It would be a long painful moment before he could breath again. He felt dizzy and his ears rang.

The big man crouched near him. "Little fishy ain't learning. You think with that pretty face you get to break the rules. Learn the code, bitch. Guy don't want to talk with you? Don't talk with the guy."

Manny was picked up and thrown back the way he came. He kept his feet as oxygen trickled back into his lungs.

He returned to his cell, face aching and confidence wobbling. He held his stomach and gingerly climbed the bunk.

Ignacio, eying the purpling mark on his cheek said, "You were only gone two minutes."

"Well, hombre," groaned Manny. "I work quick."

THAT NIGHT, after the count and lights out, Ignacio snored and Manny powered on his phone. He turned off the vibration for notifications, coming through in a rush.

More messages from Special Agent Weaver and Marshal Warren. None from Beck.

He experienced a stab of guilt. Beck had a right to feel betrayed and hurt and ignored. By now she'd told Weaver about Catalina García's brother in prison and they'd guessed that's where he was. Agents would be monitoring the prison Friday, with the intention of nabbing Catalina or tailing Rafael.

If Manny had no further information to provide, all this would be for nothing. And he had a sneaking suspicion that El Gato, one of the world's foremost troublemakers, would not be snared so easily.

As he stared at the ceiling, he got another text.

>> Hola, migo. I assume you're at some exclusive spa, getting your body hair waxed. Because you are a sissy girl.

>> I got a call from Sheriff Stackhouse. OWS downtown. I'll get her out and buy her some food tomorrow, unless you show up first.

>> Stackhouse says you're in hot water with your supervisor.

>> After you get fired, you can work at Hardees and learn how to properly grill burgers.

>> Text me if you need anything. I'm there.

Manny grinned at the message from Mackenzie August, his roommate. OWS was their code word for Old

Woman Sofia, the homeless Hispanic lady he ate breakfast with. She'd been picked up by the police again. Tomorrow morning, Mack would collect her and do his best. She was kinda sweet on Mack, anyway.

Text me if you need anything. I'm there.

He would be, too. Anything Manny needed. The way their friendship worked, picking each other up from prison didn't seem that far-fetched.

He replied, **Thanks, Mack. I owe you.**

Tell Stackhouse hot water is my favorite water.

Home in a few days.

He laid down the phone and listened to men on the far side of the cell block shout.

His aching face kept him awake two more hours.

Twenty-two Years Earlier

MANUEL MARTINEZ COULDN'T FALL asleep. The other prisoners weren't even trying; they stayed up laughing and smoking, shaking his flimsy rusted bunk when they fell against it. He needed sleep so bad it made him cry.

He was only thirteen, he shouldn't be in the same cell as these men. The administration would discover the error soon—he prayed. But who cared about a nothing little boy? So many reeking bodies in such a small space. His heart pounded until it hurt his ears.

He stared at the broken cement ceiling of Complejo Correciónal Las Cucharas, in Puerto Rico, and felt he was at the very bottom of the world, with all its great weight bearing down to crush him.

Nineteen Years Earlier

MANNY WATCHED America slide under the plane's starboard wing. He tried to wake his mom to see the beaches, but she wouldn't. Empty bottles of airplane liquor spilled from her lap when she moved.

The young stewardess arrived to clean up the bottles. She winked at Manny, the third time she'd done so.

He was seventeen. He'd paid for the plane tickets himself, money earned from fighting, his knuckles still raw. He also paid for her Immigrant Visa, secured the sponsorship from his uncle, and submitted the paperwork.

America. Freedom. Hope.

Tears streamed down his face. He was never leaving again. He'd do whatever it took.

The plastic top of the seat's armrest broke, he was squeezing it so hard.

That night in Cell Block B he fell asleep with the phone on. An incoming message activated the screen and its bright light woke him. It was one in the morning.

>> Do you know why people are attracted to you, Manuel Martinez?

>> Of course, your handsome face helps. But it's more than that.

>> It's because you have hope. You constantly smile. Our world is difficult and rough and it grinds us down. You know this more than most. And yet...you are in good spirits. Always.

>> Your resilience is one reason I think of you so often.

>> That, and you beat two of my guardians with a formal dining chair. I've been fantasizing about that since.

>> Are you hiding?

>> Where oh where are you, my love?

Without having to be told, he knew the unknown number belonged to Catalina. She was texting in Spanish.

You tell me first.

>> You aren't at your house.

>> You aren't at your office.

>> Are you looking for me? I am flattered...and, yes I'll say it, aroused.

He rubbed his bleary eyes.

His secret was still safe. She didn't know where he was. If she did, she'd be taunting him about being in jail.

You could make my job a lot easier. Give me your location.

>> I'm no longer at the palace.

I know. I made sure of that.

>> And if I tell you, will you come here?

Yes.

>> And what would we do?

He slid the phone under the thin wool blanket as a guard walked by with the brightest flashlight ever built. After pausing to listen for the guard's retreat, he pulled it out again and dimmed the screen's brightness.

We would go to bed together. Like we did a lifetime ago, as kids.

>> And then?

And then I would arrest you.

>> Oooh, with cuffs, I hope.

>> Manuel, my heart, you know your police cannot catch me. So instead, please, join us.

>> I won't wait forever.

When do you leave?

A longer pause. Then...

>> Saturday.

32

The guard with the flashlight returned at 4:30am. Manny rolled out of bed, hungry and raw and tired, like he was made of rust, and he said every curse word he knew in English.

The guy behind the blinding light said, "This says you go by Sinatra?"

Manny nodded and yawned. Scrubbed his chin. He needed a shave.

"But that's not your real name."

"Maybe. Maybe not. I do it my way."

"Clever. Let's go, Sinatra, you're cooking breakfast for all these fine gentlemen."

Ignacio never stirred.

This early, the walk across the lawn reminded him of turning off a shower—a sudden rush of chill and loneliness. A handful of other guys trudged with him, heads down. He stamped his foot to restore full sensation to his leg.

Two detention officers let them into the kitchen one at a time, subjecting each to a strip search. They called him Pretty Boy and the inspection was rigorous and thorough.

Compared to the basketball courts and the bathrooms and lockers, the kitchen struck Manny as pristine. Commercial grade galvanized steel appliances and mopped floors and racks of cooking utensils. A head chef bawled orders and inmates moved like sleep walkers, fetching ingredients from muscle memory.

Rafael García moved through the kitchen without affecting it. He had no responsibilities and even the head chef seemed to recognize his *otherness*. Rafael was only here because he had to be, but he would not cook. And no one dared ask him. Compared to the other men in the kitchen, Rafael was shockingly handsome. He eventually amused himself by drying mixing bowls coming out of the washer.

Today they cooked oatmeal re-rack. Manny stirred the oatmeal with a steel paddle as another man added small portions of hot water and margarine. No one called him Sinatra. He was Pretty Boy or New Fish.

After thirty minutes of work, Rafael strolled close.

Manny said, "So you go by Arroyo now."

Two inmates stepped between them. Like they'd been ready. The shorter of the two, a man with only one eye, raised a metal spatula to Manny's throat and said, "*No le hablas, perra.*"

For the first time, Rafael made eye contact with him. His expression didn't change but he arched an eyebrow.

Manny debated taking the spatula and gouging the man's remaining eye. But he raised his hands in surrender. Before he turned back to the oatmeal, he said, "Cute name, Arroyo. That's not what I called you in Los Angeles. You forget your old friends."

He grabbed the paddle and stirred again.

Rafael didn't reply. From the corner of his eye, Manny could see him drying with the rag. Thinking and drying, and looking his way occasionally.

MANNY STOOD in line for the shower for an hour before lunch, saving a spot for Ignacio. Cell Block B had only two showers and the line boggled the mind. Ignacio arrived to take his spot and the men behind made no complaint—this was common practice. Ignacio paid for the favor with a bowl of Ramen noodles, which Manny heated and devoured. He still didn't trust the gathering at the chow hall.

He went to the yard again during lunch. The same small guys were there, walking and exercising under the broiling July sun.

The buzzer rang and most of Cell Block B exited into the yard in a controlled mass movement, a sea of yellow. Manny stayed on the track, keeping his distance from Bill Wolfe and Chilly the Kid and other faces he remembered.

Rafael began his circuit of the track, walking proud with hands clasped behind. His gaze found Manny and he closed the distance. They met at the farthest point in the yard, away from the crowd.

Rafael spoke in Spanish.

"You will be killed later today."

Manny said, "About time."

"Unless I call it off. You knew me in Los Angeles? What did you call me?" He spoke softly and Manny did too.

"I called you Rafael Gará in Los Angeles. So did

everyone else. I knew your sister, Catalina. Last time I saw you was at Scotty's. You left soon after for Honduras."

Rafael nodded. He twisted to look at the mob around the basketball court, then to his two body guards, then back to Manny. He nodded again. "Okay."

"We worked together."

"We worked together," repeated Rafael. He stuck out his hand and Manny shook it. A truce struck. "You look familiar. But I don't remember the details."

"Forget about it. It's been ten years. I don't even remember what people called *me* then."

Rafael pointed at Manny's face, an accumulating mess of swollen bruises and burns. "Sorry about your face. My man did that."

"I broke the code. I knew the rules. But I wanted to speak with you. Whatever you got going on here, I want in," said Manny.

"You want in."

"Yes but I get out in two weeks. I'm only here because of a prisoner transfer thing, a screw up," said Manny. "The guards, they don't know their ass from apple butter."

"Two weeks," repeated Rafael.

"Yes."

"Good. I'm glad for you. But I'm gone tomorrow."

Manny expressed surprise. "Tomorrow? Walking free?"

"I'll talk to Santiago before I go. Tell the guys to back down. See if you can be of use the next two weeks."

"Where are you going? I won't be far behind, leaving this place," said Manny. "And I liked working with the García family."

Rafael chuckled. "In two weeks? By then I'll be the President of Panama. Or dead."

He said it as a joke but Manny heard the truth underneath. His ears rang. President of Panama.

Rafael said, "Stay out of trouble. Obey the code, Sinatra, and the guys will let you be." He turned to continue his walk. "I like that name, by the way."

That night, after lights out, Manny turned on his phone again. A rush of messages from Beck waited.

>> Okay, I did some research on Panama. The country is in election season.

>> There's a growing swell of support for a right-wing revolutionary party, led by Ricardo Herrera. But no one's seen Herrera for months.

>> I bet you a dollar that Ricardo Herrera is another alias of Rafael Garcia.

>> Ricardo is expected to make a dramatic appearance soon and potentially swing the election.

>> I spoke with a contact in the US Department of Foreign affairs, and they fear the right-wing revolutionary wing plans a congressional coup, with the intention of altering the constitution, no matter the results.

>> And yes, that's almost exactly what happened in Honduras ten years ago.

>> I think Rafael Garcia was telling the truth.

Manny's head swam. Just how influential *was*

Catalina? She was about to topple a second government? Or was it a third?

>> Yesterday I was sure you were fired.

>> But now, after passing the Panama news to Weaver, I detect a glimmer of hope. =)

>> And possibly I'll get a promotion, which is far more important.

>> Additional agencies are getting in on this. You uncovered something big. A week ago, they didn't want to risk a stand-off with El Gato. But grabbing her, plus Rafael Garcia/Ricardo Herrera is a no-brainer.

>> Rafael will be tailed by aerial assets when he leaves tomorrow. Ideally he'll lead us directly to El Gato. Otherwise, we're prepping to make the arrest at the airport.

>> Just tell me this...

>> Why did you go into the prison without my help?

>> Some banal reason having to do with male pride and insufficiency issues, I bet.

Good question, Beck. He had several answers.

One, he knew Weaver would forbid it and that Beck was a rule follower. So he couldn't tell her.

Two, he liked Noelle Beck. More than he liked most people, and he didn't want her injured or fired.

Three...male pride and insufficiency issues. Catalina was a deeply personal issue for him.

Manny lowered the phone when he heard footsteps. Part of him wanted to call Allan Johnston now. Wake him up and get the hell out of his jail cell. And yet...

...he still didn't believe that Catalina and Rafael would be caught so easily. Powerful men and women don't get that way by being naive and uninformed.

No, he couldn't leave yet. Rafael was scheduled for

release tomorrow, but when? Manny might have one more shot at him in the kitchen. But for what reason? To get more information?

Or to assassinate him with a paddle. He liked both options.

The approaching footsteps stopped at his cell door. He heard a squeaking sound and a thump— someone had opened and sat in a metal chair outside his cell.

He rose on the top bunk, peering out the security window.

The walkway and common areas were partially lit even this late. The man sitting outside in the chair nodded and said, "Good evening, Mr. Martinez."

It was Hubert, the steward of the Appalachian Palace. The hairs on Manny's arms pressed against the jumpsuit he still wore.

"*Beunos noches*, Hubert. You here for a conjugal visit?"

The man smiled. Polite and brief. "For the sake of your cell mate, let's keep our voices down. It'd be better for Ignacio's health if he remained asleep."

"I understand."

"You can imagine my surprise, Mr. Martinez, to find you here."

"Imagine my surprise, amigo, at being found."

"The underworld, as it's often called, is vast. I am a small part but I have access to its unimaginable resources and information."

"What, like a villain newsletter?"

Hubert smiled again and struck Manny once more as a kind, friendly old man. "More or less. Do you know why I came here, instead of simply requesting you be made to disappear, Mr. Martinez?"

"Because I didn't shoot you in Harlan."

Hubert raised his fingers. "There are two reasons. That is the first. You spared my life and thus I feel compelled to return the favor. We are gentlemen, after all, even if our world is bloodthirsty. Most of my guests are...blunt and brutish, or spoiled and entitled. I find you strike the appropriate chord, Mr. Martinez, between cultured and cutthroat. A rarity."

Manny debated telling Hubert that he preferred to be called Machiavellian, but balked. He might be requested to define it. Also, he was experiencing an emotion uncommon for him—fear.

"Second, and more importantly, I want to know why you are here."

Manny's mind churned. Did Hubert not know about Rafael? Did Catalina never tell him? For all of Hubert's resources, he appeared ignorant.

He asked, "Why's that matter, Hubert?"

"Did you know federal agents are crawling through my home as we speak?"

"They won't find anything incriminating."

"Of course not. But the establishment I operate is absolutely reliant upon discretion and secrecy. You've already cost me credibility with my future guests, you understand. Repairing our reputation could take years. I need to know if your current endeavors present a further threat to me or Catalina García."

"I'm a US Marshal," Manny replied quietly. "You think the only thing I got going on is the Catalina affair?"

"Tell me why you are here, Mr. Martinez. The only plank you and I proceed on is mutual respect."

"I'm here to surveil."

Hubert made an 'And?' motion with his hand. He needed more.

Manny said, "I'm telling you nothing else, Hubert. The mutual respect isn't infinite. I busted you and your men tried to kill me. We're even, I think, and now I'm onto something else. You want to avoid additional trouble from the feds? Take off and forget I'm here."

Hubert regarded him silently for a full minute. Manny took the chance to slow his pulse and clear his mind. He needed rational thought, not panic.

Hubert said finally, "I don't believe you."

"I don't care, *ese*. Surely, as a card carrying member of the underworld, you understand the need for secrecy."

"Why are you here?"

"Not your business."

"I see." Hubert stood and collected his chair. "You have a reputation, Mr. Martinez. As an officer of the law who abuses prisoners under your care."

"You heard wrong. I abuse criminals *before* they become prisoners. When they can still fight back."

"Yet still, this warning seems appropriate. Good luck." He nodded and walked off.

Manny's stomached twisted. A feeling of dread.

Boots outside his cell. His door clanged and opened. The loudest sound he'd ever heard. Men came in with high-powered flashlights.

"Inmate Sinatra," said the first detention officer. He sneered the name. "We got orders to move you. Let's go."

Move him. A disaster.

Prison is a violent and cruel world. And sometimes my staff is worse than the inmates, said the warden.

Manny held up his hands. "Amigos. It's important I stay in this cell. And not move." Even as he uttered the syllables, he knew they landed like bags of concrete at his feet, not remotely connecting with their ears.

He cleared his throat and tried again.

I'm a federal marshal with a Supremacy License. I have a phone in my bed and I cannot leave because I need access to it. I'm departing the prison tomorrow but before then I need to squeeze one of your prisoners for more information. Or maybe kill him. So let's all go to sleep and forget this. And don't tell anyone. Especially not the other prisoners.

None of that came out, because it'd get him killed. What actually came out of his mouth, "I'm not moving."

"Yeah. You are."

"It'll take all of you."

The guards laughed. The closest guy clicked his taser and an arc of blue electricity flickered in his fist. Manny had been tased before. He preferred to avoid it.

He raised his hand to block a beam of flashlight and he said, "Hey. You. You're the bartender. And a night guard?" It was the gorilla who tended bar in Gate City, the man who called him José and made a poor whiskey sour.

The gorilla chuckled. "You're the spic who threw his drink at me."

"Yeah. It was awful. So...use your brain, gorilla night guard. I was in your bar. Now I'm here. Bet you can figure out why I need to stay in this cell."

The blue lightening crackled again.

The man said, "Bet you can figure out where I'm gonna shove this taser, José."

"As long as it's made in America, señor."

They laughed again. Two more guards squeezed into the cell. Four against one.

"You'll get me," he said, voice strong. "I admit it, you

guys are too fat. I can't beat you all. But it'll cost you broken noses now and broken careers later."

"Worth it."

"Mind if I make a phone call real quick?"

They advanced.

Manny kicked the guy's hand. The hand lurched upwards, jabbing the taser into his own fat neck. Blue sparked. The fat detention officer made a sound, half a scream and half rolling his R's, tumbling backwards, Manny following, stepping up the electrocuted officer like a foot ladder. Quick punches, as a boxer would, Manny snapping fists and elbows into faces and throats before they could react. The gorilla falling with a broken nose, dropping his flashlight.

A can of mace hissed and emitted a thick stream of pungent OC spray. Bottled agony. The stream caught Manny in the ear and forehead, and drenched the bartender.

Manny leaped for the door but they caught him by the waist. His fingers grabbing the doorway, eyes filling, and he gagged. So did the detention officers. OC spray, awful stuff.

"But really," he wheezed. "I need to stay in this cell. Let's be cool, amigos."

They didn't release. Manny desperate now, smashing his elbow into the closest officer's face, bruising his olecranon bone and destroying the man's cartilage. Again and again.

Someone inside the cell vomited. He hoped it wasn't Ignacio. The OC fog was thick and rolling out of the doorway.

He squirmed free outside the cell and pulled himself

up on the railing. The general population was awake and alert to the mayhem. Shouting and calling.

Rooting for Manny.

It's the inmates versus the guards.

Convicts versus cops, that's the code.

But I'm a cop!

More lights came on with heavy clangs. Guards running through doors and charging the stairs.

He'd never get his phone now. Four fat inmates were in his way, even if they could barely breathe.

Manny hopped the railing, lowered himself fist over fist like a hand ladder, and dropped the remaining two feet to the second floor railing. He landed in a crouched perch, only just keeping his balance, and went over again. Hand over hand, until hanging by his fingertips. He released and fell the six feet to the common area floor.

The guards on the third floor gaped at him. They couldn't do *that*.

All his time in the gym, paying off.

"Sinatra, *imbécil*, the game is up," he told himself. Did he have options? Escape from a level five state prison? Doubtful—this prison was made in America, after all. Hide? Meh. He needed Norris or Johnston. Lead the guards away, circle back for the phone, and call for—

An electroshock device pressed firmly below his hairline and activated. An alligator biting his neck, he felt like. A tornado funnel opening in his head. Sticking his face into an industrial 220 volt outlet.

He lost muscular control. The world hit reset, turned white, and blinked back on in reverse.

He was on the ground, looking up, twitching.

The face of Norris hovered over him. His patchy beard was bad. His green eye was brighter than the blue.

"My, my, inmate *Sinatra*. You ain't doing too well, huh."

34

The guards took turns beating him with riot batons, cracking his ribs. His lip split and both lower bicuspids on the left side loosened. He ignored the pain, the way he'd learned as a child. Getting hurt wasn't the worst thing in the world, he knew. The teeth would refasten and ribs would knit. Retreat inside and return later to heal.

He was taken to the basement of Cell Block C and thrown roughly into a solitary confinement cell. It was the size of a small bathroom and he hit the wall hard. He watched Norris in the doorway through his good eye—the other would swell shut soon. Norris should have been his contact to the outside world, yet the man had participated in the beating. His loyalty had shifted.

"Norris." Manny's words slurred. "You work for Hubert?"

"A dumbass question, Sinatra. I know the man, sure. But we both get paid by the powers that be. Know what I mean?"

"You work with the underworld."

"Call it what you like."

"You tell him why I'm here?"

Norris snorted. "I don't know why you're here. Told him you were snooping around."

"Whatever they're paying you, it's not worth it."

"Worth what?"

"Defiling the sanctity of America."

A laugh. "The horse shit that comes out of your mouth."

"It's not worth treason. You talked with Johnston, you know who I am. This is national security."

"Down here? There is no American government. They don't know and don't care what happens here. They give us keys for a reason, Sinatra. Keep guys in, yeah. But also it keeps them out, cause there's things they don't wanna know."

Manny got to his feet. Winced, held his ribs.

"I need to talk to Johnston."

"Johnston ain't here, boy."

"The American government's gonna tear you apart, Norris."

"You're in hell, Marshal. It ain't me you should be worried about."

The door clanged home.

35

The bodily damage wasn't significant. No permanent injuries. Two or three weeks tops, good to go. He'd conquered pain before.

The worst part was, Catalina would get on a plane and leave. Again. And topple a country in Central America. Again. The American government was underestimating her.

He stared at the ceiling, listening to the sounds from the bottom of the world. Nearby prisoners shrieked to ease the boredom. Over his head he detected the thump and bang of doors. Distant words blared through the PA system.

His mental clock kept time. No one brought him breakfast. By lunch time he guessed Rafael García had been released, a free man.

How ironic.

No food until dinner; a tray of over boiled green beans and fish goop slid through the slot. He'd need to be a lot hungrier before he tried that mess.

He was lost in the system, he knew. Norris would take

his time submitting the transfer paperwork because no one would ask. And by the time Johnston or Beck or someone came for him Norris would feign ignorance and help look, but Manny'd be dead.

This kinda thing happened. A lot. There were a million ways for the system to abuse criminals.

Somewhere deep inside his chest, Manny felt a pang of guilt. He had a reputation for being rough with the men he chased. He bragged about it, felt he was doing good. He didn't believe in warnings and the criminals certainly deserved punishment. Being on the other side of the violence, however, it seemed less noble.

The walls closed in and he couldn't sleep. Hour by hour he diminished in his own eyes. Confidence shot, he lost his mind trying to keep track of time. Was it midnight? Four in the morning? He'd been in here his whole life. Solitary madness and failure crept in through his nose and ears, until he finally dozed...

THEY CAME FOR HIM. He didn't know how long he'd been asleep. It was morning, Saturday, he bet.

The door opened. Guards with mace cautiously entered, ready to blast him. Cans held out like a shield, batons raised. He stood and a hooked rod pinioned him face first to the painted cinderblock by his neck. They held the mace on him and cuffed his wrists.

Two guards marched him down a hall with low ceilings under the watch of Norris. Walking the green mile, he knew. A death march, his final minutes.

"Take the cuffs off, Norris," he said. "Let's settle this like men."

"How's that?"

"You choose. Arm wrestling? Thumb war?"

Norris didn't answer. His lips were pressed firm. He looked gray and he sweated.

"Let me go and I still have time to stop an international terrorist."

"You know," said one of the guards. "If your eye weren't busted, if your lips weren't split, if your face wasn't mostly purple and green, you might be the prettiest man I ever saw."

"Cut the carbs," replied Manny. "It'll help."

"Shut it, Davis," Norris snapped. "Let's get this over with."

They led him to the bathroom. Not the showers, those were separate. Again a rod was used to pinion him face first against the cold wall and his cuffs were removed. The guard pocketed them and the pressure eased enough for him to rotate.

"Now strip."

"Norris, now's not the time for flirting."

Norris smiled nervously without humor. "You need to wash up. Take off the jumpsuit."

Manny, still pinned to the wall by his neck with the eight-foot rod, grinned. His lip partially split open again. "Maybe you come here and make me."

Norris took a can of mace from the second guard. Shook it and came close enough to aim directly at Manny's uninjured eye.

"This is happening, Sinatra. You wanna take off the jumpsuit? Or you want mace in your eye and then take off the jumpsuit?"

"There a third option?"

"I could fire a taser at your balls. *Then* mace you. *Then* make you strip."

"Norris, you had a disturbed childhood, I think." But Manny didn't want to absorb an eyeful of OC spray so he unzipped. Wiggled until the jumpsuit fell to his ankles, then stepped onto the legs to pull free as best he could while pinned by the neck. The slippers on his feet tugged loose.

"Now," said Norris and he licked his lips. "Get on in there and wash up. We'll wait here."

"What's in the bathroom, Norris?"

"Only what you deserve. Get on."

They took no chances. The pinion rod scraped against the wall, guiding Manny into the doorway. The guard kept steady pressure, pushing him down the short hall that opened into the bathroom behind the wall. Two sinks. Two toilets. And four inmates.

Bill Wolfe stood at the sink with another white supremacist. Plus Chilly the Kid and a second Latino bruiser. They had unzipped their jumpsuits down to the waist and tied the arms like a belt. Each man outweighed him by fifty pounds.

He'd be beaten to death by the very men he put here. Poetry.

"Look who it is," said Wolfe. He chuckled, dark circles under his eyes. His bald head glinted. One of his tattoos was a swastika. "It's the spic, ol' Man-well Martinez. Man-well the marshal."

Chilly the Kid held up his fingers. His tattoos were branded on and raised. "You remember me, *policia?* You broke my finger in the door. Know what I'm gonna do to you? To each one of your got'damn fingers?"

Manny shrugged. "You killed two girlfriends with those fingers, Chilly, is what the jury decided."

"Gonna see how long we can make this last, marshal. Make it till lunch before you bleed out."

Manny held up a hand. "First, though, *por favor*, I got an idea."

He moved, sudden and quick. Snagged the rod still pressing into his neck and tugged it out of the startled guard's grip. Manny spun it like a staff and caught Chilly near the eye. Norris shouting. Chilly fell backwards and Manny shoved the pinion hook into Wolfe's face. The hook didn't go round his neck, but the left point inserted into the man's open mouth. Wolfe falling, gagging, hands on the rod and ripping it from Manny.

The two inmates Manny didn't know came for him. He needed space.

Manny bolted from the bathroom and dove for the floor at the guards' boots. Trying to slide through. Jets of OC spray arced over him, missing. The floor wasn't slick; he didn't slide—his skin caught and he rolled into their legs.

A tangle on the floor now.

Sheer weight subdued Manny. Pinned beneath hundreds of pounds, he couldn't breathe. Convict and guard working in unison against a common enemy. His wrists and ankles were grabbed and he was lifted up. Carried by each appendage back toward the bathroom.

He struggled. Useless. Out of time, out of options.

Then there was a woman.

She shouted. "Hold it!"

Then a man's voice. "What the *hell* is happening?"

Beck and Allan Johnston came through the doorway from the stairwell, like a couple entering a nightmare.

Johnston wore jeans and a short-sleeved flannel shirt—Beck had rousted him from home and it looked like she hadn't slept.

Manny chuckled but it hurt. "The fellas and I are bathing each other. It's my turn."

"Norris..." Johnston, black eyes drilling, didn't know what to say. "Explain."

Norris declined. He ran a tongue along his lower teeth. A man weighing his options.

Beck smoothly undid the strap on her holster and drew her service Glock. She saw the same thing Manny saw—Johnston's authority over the situation wasn't guaranteed.

No cameras down here. Four violent inmates out of their cages. And Norris suddenly staring at jail time if he laid down. Indecision balanced on a knife.

Manny was dropped to the floor.

Allan Johnston snapped, "Davis, Barton, escort the prisoners to their cell block."

David and Barton, holding riot batons and mace, glanced at each other and at Norris. Murmured, "Yes sir," but they didn't move.

This place was hell, Norris had said. And he took money from the underworld. The guards could be worse than the inmates.

Lives on a scale, bobbing up and down.

"Beck," Manny said and he nodded at Norris. "He's the one. He's with APOG."

She understood. She held the only firearm. And Norris stood as their leader.

"Lay down," she ordered. Strong voice. In a Weaver stance. Glaring down the sight at Norris. "On the ground. Now."

"Lady, who the hell—"

She shot him. A single round, passing under the outermost layers of flesh on his left thigh. The blast wrecked their ears; the slug pinged off the wall. Norris flopped onto the floor tile and screamed. Crimson pooled under.

She turned the gun onto the inmates.

"Davis, Barton, move!" Johnston roared.

Under the threat of her gun, the guards shouted orders at the inmates and the circus moved toward the stairwell. Wolfe, his mouth bleeding, and Chilly glaring at Manny. Johnston took a pair of cuffs from Davis. He triggered his radio and kept up the shouting, relaying orders. He got on his knees near Norris and snapped on a cuff. The might of the American government swinging into place.

"Norris, damn it," he said. "What in the *hell*."

Norris whimpered.

Manny moved to the corner, panting, and rested a moment on top of his puddled jumpsuit. His head dropped back against the wall. "Beck." He panted. Felt like a rib was stuck in his lung. "The most beautiful señorita alive."

Beck lowered her gun. The barrel quavered and so did her voice. "Good grief, Sinatra."

"Not bad for a computer nerd, Beck."

"You have a lot of tattoos."

"I used to be impulsive." He winked. "Partner."

"Don't 'partner' me," she said. "And get your ass up."

36

Manny dressed in the vacant office of the warden. *Ay caramba*, that man would have a macabre report waiting when he returned from Disney.

He came out, adjusting his belt with the silver buckle. He had missed his clothes, even if his shirt was torn and burnt. Matched the rest of him. Glock at the small of his back, revolver under his arm.

Beck waited in the outer office; it was Saturday and the warden's assistant hadn't come in. She indicated his face. "You look awful."

"Mean guys hit me."

"We lost Rafael yesterday. FBI had a Hawk Owl in the air but he never showed. We think he had inside help; he waited until daylight and went through the woods and got picked up a couple miles away. I personally planted a tracker inside his jacket hem but we found it discarded near the door."

Manny cursed, though this didn't surprise him. They left the hard world of concrete walls and moved into the parking lot.

She tapped her ear and kept talking. "I'm getting constant updates through bluetooth. An hour ago a state trooper spotted a caravan headed north on Interstate 81. Four black Toyota sedans with tinted windows. We sent it to MASINT and now we've got a plane shadowing the caravan two miles out. Right on schedule with the private flight out of Roanoke. Our Marshals are waiting at the airport. So are the FBI's special operations and surveillance groups."

Manny didn't reply. He walked a circle around his Camaro, a muscle in his jaw flexing. "That easy, huh."

"Easy? Jeez, Sinatra, you've been half killed the past few days. *Several* times."

"Catalina gets in a car, lets the feds watch her the whole way, and waltzes into a trap. It's that easy?"

Beck raised her hands, palms up. "There will be a shoot-out or standoff. Make you feel better? I should be there, you know—participating, instead of rescuing your impetuous behind from solitary confinement."

"I'm embarrassed the Marshals are being duped. The FBI? Sure, fine. But not us. She's not in the caravan."

Beck didn't respond. Watched him pace, hands on his hips. It was hot; she started to sweat in the July bake.

He said, "It's a decoy. A distraction and it worked. Every cop, marshal, and agent in three hundred miles is at that damn airport."

"What do you want—"

"Are there any airstrips nearby?"

"Out *here?*"

"Check. On your phone. Mine's long gone."

She punched her screen with her thumbs. Sighed. Waited for the poor reception to catch up. "Yes, there's a tiny airstrip called Powell Valley, five miles away."

"Too close to the jail. Too risky. Zoom out."

"Okay, fine...one sec...right, yes, Lonesome Pine. It's more like a private airport than a mere landing strip. Probably for dusting crops and recreational flights. Guys with prop jets and pilot licenses to impress their friends, I bet."

"How far?"

She squinted at her screen. "Twenty-two miles. Get this, geographically it forms an elongated triangle with the Palace and the prison."

"That's it." He banged his palm on the Camaro's roof. "Get in."

"We're going to Lonesome Pine Airport?"

"El Gato might be there. Got something better to do, Beck?"

"Marshal Warren wants us back in Roanoke. *Pronto.*"

"Catalina's not at Lonesome Pine? We'll go back."

"What about my car?"

"It's a government issue. Someone else will come get it. You're too valuable to fret about things like that. Let's *go.*" He opened his door.

She did too. Pleased.

HALFWAY THERE, as Manny screamed tight around country roads, Beck said, "Penis."

"Say again?"

"I saw your penis." Her eyes were closed and she rubbed at her forehead. "In the basement."

"Uh oh. Your faith in Mormonism wobbling?"

"No. But I've never been good at it." She lowered her head into her hands. "My local LDS congregation is...flexible. I didn't even do the eighteen-month mission out of college."

"You just shot a guy in the leg, *señorita*. Shouldn't that bother you more?"

"I was saving a life. Somehow I'm feeling more conviction from the Heavenly Mother about seeing...I need to confess it and move on."

"No can do, Beck. Gonna remind you every morning. You're a virgin, aren't you. I'm impressed cause you're kinda hot."

She said, "That doesn't matter. What matters—thank you—what matters is my internal convictions. And I choose to wait. So this is a loss of innocence moment, because I don't have much experience with naked men."

"You picked a good one to start with."

"I confessed it to you. I cleared the air. Now we move on, as professionals."

"Are you thinking about it right now?"

"Focus Sinatra."

37

Beck stayed quiet the rest of the trip, listening to chatter in her earpiece. Five miles from the Lonesome Pine she said, "El Gato's caravan has reached Roanoke's airport. The Marshals and the FBI are surrounding it on the tarmac." Her eyes looked far off to the horizon, like she could almost see it over the hill.

Manny nodded. He wanted her arrested. He wanted her to be in those cars. But he doubted it.

"No shots fired yet," she muttered. "That's good."

A mile from the Lonesome Pine, roaring up 644. Manny moved it over a hundred on the straightaways.

She caught her breath. Listened. Said, "Oh crud."

"What?"

"The Marshal's Special Operations Group just turned infrared and parabolic mics on the windows. Cars are empty except for the drivers."

"Damn it," said Manny. But he *knew* they would be.

"...team moving in. ...drivers stepping out of cars. ... you're right, it was a decoy."

Manny nodded. Catalina was at the airport coming into view. Had to be.

"And just like that, our government is humiliated. Once again."

Manny said, "Not if we catch her. Marshals still got time to save the day."

"I'm not a marshal. I'm NSA."

"You're deputized, señorita. You ride with me."

"Why're we doing this, Sinatra? Because it's our job? Or because you love her?"

"I do *not* love Catalina García."

"I mean, is it business or personal?"

"It's deeply personal. She's not getting on another plane to destroy a country."

The last time, she'd left his personal life in shambles. This time, she'd be leaving his professional life wrecked. If he caught her he felt both could be salvaged somehow.

But what would he do with her? Send her to jail for the rest of her life? Kill her? He hated both options.

Lonesome Pine rests in a vast field hidden by thick forests. They came up 723 and the airport opened—the terminal was the size of a large house, fronted by a cracked parking lot, and behind was the unmistakably flat land of a long runway.

Three cars sat in the parking lot—one was a black Lexus. Manny's heart skipped a beat. The Camaro slid to a stop in a stink of brakes, perpendicular to the Lexus, pinning it in. He got out, Glock drawn, and shouted for Catalina.

The car remained still. Not a tremor.

He came around his door and banged on the window.

"Ay! Open the door!"

"Careful! What if they shoot?" called Beck.

"Bullet proof glass. They can't."

The window then buzzed smoothly down. Manny pointed the barrel of his pistol into the widening gap and pinned himself to the rear door. He peered into the exposed driver seat.

The handsome face of Hubert.

He removed a pair of tortoiseshell wayfarers and smiled. "Mr. Martinez, I am surprised. A Camaro? A loud and preposterous machine, yet you dress with obvious relish and class. The juxtaposition is amusing. Though at the moment your face and shirt match the vehicle."

"Good hell, Hubert, you're too big with us."

"You mean ubiquitous, I think. My profession requires it."

Beck came around the car, gun trained on the Lexus's open window. "Hubert? This is *the* Hubert?"

"Good morning, Noelle Beck," he said. "The pleasure is mine. A gun? The rumors are true; you're promoted to 1811."

Her face paled; he knew her name and profession.

Manny cast a glance at the terminal. "You're here, *hombre*. Which means Catalina's inside."

"Once again, Mr. Martinez, you're a minute too late."

Hidden behind the terminal, a plane's engine coughed to life. A lonely sound, soaked by the forest.

Beck asked, "We're arresting this guy, right?"

"For what, my dear?"

"Aiding and abetting a felony. Not to mention the massacre—"

"Come, come, Ms. Beck. You're in the big leagues now. That'd be a waste of both our time. Your inspection of my establishment has been fruitless. Plus, will they accept the testimony of disgraced US Deputy Marshal Manuel

Martinez? No, I'm afraid in this case it's either shoot me or I leave."

The pitch of the airplane's engine roar changed. The sound bounced off different surfaces as it taxied.

Manny lowered his Glock. "C'mon, Beck. He's right about one thing—we're not after him, a mere hotel manager and delivery driver."

Hubert laughed and slipped on his glasses. "Ouch, Mr Martinez. And here I thought we were even. Good luck to you both."

"He killed five deputy marshals," Beck reminded Manny. "We let him leave?"

"He was following orders. Plus, we know where he lives. Another day, we'll get him. *Vamonos!*" He started jogging around the terminal, toward the sound of the engine. Toward Catalina. The security gate stood open near the large fuel tanks. Beck followed him.

The lane opened into a wide lot, mostly empty. At the far end of the parking lot a white and yellow King Air 90, a twin-engine plane used by skydivers, glinted in the sun. Manny jogged the distance, his vision centered on his gun's sight and the plane.

But that wasn't Catalina's ride, he realized. She wouldn't fly away on a jump plane. Plus, the propellers weren't turning.

A second plane came into view, distant, beyond the white hanger. A turboprop, a little red Cessna, already on the runway, propeller a humming blur. At this range he saw no details inside the cabin but Catalina and Rafael had to be inside. The Cessna paused in pre-threshold and throttled up. Brakes released and it rumbled up the center line. Manny ran and he shouted but it was worthless—the

Cessna was a quarter mile away. He raised the Glock...absurd.

The plane accumulated speed, faster, faster, lifted at the touchdown, and plunged into the blue.

There she goes. Again.

"Hey, hey, hey, what's a matter?" shouted a man, coming round the King Air 90. He had the rangy confidence most skydivers possess. Face and hair permanently windblown. He noted their firearms and raised his hands. "Whoa."

Manny pointed. "Who's on the plane?"

"Eerrr, I forget the names." His hands were still up. "Spanish names I can't remember, no offense. What's a matter?"

"A man and a women? Both Hispanic?"

"That's right. Gorgeous people, too," said the man. "What's going on?"

Beck flashed her credentials. "Federal agents. You rented a plane to international terrorists."

"Gotta be kidding me. His pilot's license checked out. Jezz, well, I'm sorry, but they'll be back soon. Only reserved it an hour."

"They aren't coming back," Manny said. His ribs hurt him and his facial contusions pulsed.

"They aren't coming back?" repeated the man. "Where do you reckon they—"

Manny slapped his hand against the King Air's tail fin. The structure thudded. "Get this plane moving, *señor*. We need to follow."

"Follow them? Gotta be kidding me," said the man again.

"What's your name?"

"Keith."

"Move your ass, Keith."

"But—"

"No time, *amigo*. We got a minute or two before that plane is out of sight."

"But what will—"

Manny raised his pistol into the air and fired it.

That's one. Eight bullets left.

"*Gee*-sus!" Keith ducked. "Okay, okay!"

"Skip the checklist. I want to be wheels up."

Keith moved quick. He had been halfway through his pre-flight warm up for a jump next hour. Manny and Beck boarded. He fired the engine cold, mixed the fuel, flipped on the master switch, throttled the engine, checked the oil pressure, and toggled the flaps up. He taxied them to the runway, which seemed to stretch to infinity.

"Okay, good to go, agents!" He shouted at them over the pulsing propellers. "Good luck! Try to bring her home in one piece, you hear? Else I'm a dead man."

Beck and Manny were in the back. Her mouth fell open.

Manny called, "*Hombre*, you're flying us."

"Hah! I ain't a pilot! I'm a jumper! They just let me do the pre-flight stuff for fun. You're on your own." He opened the pilot's door and jumped out.

"*Ay dios mio! Carajo!*" Manny swore. "You're up, Beck."

"I'm *up*? What's that mean, I'm *up*?"

"You were in the Air Force."

"I wasn't a pilot!"

"You *never* flew a plane?"

"Not really, no. I didn't get that far. My motion sickness worsened."

"You did the simulators," said Manny.

"That is *not* the same!"

"Did you crash?"

"No, but—"

Manny pointed out the cockpit windshield, at the dot in the sky. "She's getting away, Beck."

"Sinatra—"

"Okay, *I'll* fly. Tell me before we crash." He made a motion to the pilot's chair.

"No! Okay. Sweet Jesus, okay, I'll try." She climbed forward and buckled in. Clamped on a headset and handed him one too. The terminal was chattering in the speakers—she switched off the radio.

Manny's voice pumped into her ear. "Let's go!"

"Zip it! I need a minute! I have to find..." She touched the controls like a blind woman familiarizing herself and locating certain dials. "Okay. Okay. I can get us airborne. Okay." With shaking hands she increased power, watching the RPMs climb. The engine roared, the fuselage shook.

"You took off in the simulators?"

"This is much different. Keep your mouth shut, Sinatra."

The tachometer reached green. She took a deep breath. Said a prayer. Released the brake. They lurched gracelessly and she overcorrected with foot pedals, keeping the King Air centered. The runway put on speed.

Manny muttered, "Maybe this was a bad idea."

"I quit the JFIC. Hear me? After this, I quit." She scrutinized the dash. "Flaps, where are the flaps..."

Manny closed his eyes and said a prayer too. The floor jostled under his feet. *Dulce Maria*, where are the flaps?

"Here," she said, setting to takeoff position. "Okay, we're doing good."

"What else? What can I do?"

"We should be okay." Her voice stayed strong despite the advancing forest. "Landing's another story."

The oncoming trees rose like a wall. He said, "But... should we be in the air now? Because..."

"Waiting on rotation speed. I don't know what it is so we're playing it safe."

"Yeah, but..." He closed his eyes again. "Never mind, I trust you."

Bad idea.

They shot over the touchdown zone, reached the aiming point, and she pulled back on the yoke. Her heart nearly stopped—nothing happened. She pulled harder and the ground surrendered, dropping beneath the nose.

Manny's stomach dropped into his throat.

They were airborne. She aimed at the clouds.

"Okay," she said and she took turns wiping her palm on her pants. "Okay, we're up."

Manny wiped his hands too. Then pointed south west at the speck. "There she is."

"What if we can't catch them? They've got several miles on us."

"Sure we can. Hit the gas, Beck. Our Beechcraft King Air is made in America."

"What's that matter?"

He shot her a withering glance. "It matters. Plus, we have two propellers and they only have one. Simple math."

"You're lucky you're handsome," she said, keeping the throttle open wide and packing on altitude. She knew there were details she should check—the fuel mixture, the engine gauges, the oil pressure—but her hands felt glued to the yoke, her eyes to the horizon. Like they'd fall out of the sky otherwise. "What's the plan? Tail them to their destination?"

"Get right above. I'll jump on top and force them to land."

"Jump? On top of *what?*"

"Of her airplane. The Cessna."

"That's..." She took a hand off the yoke long enough to rub her eyes. She needed sunglasses—the vibrancy hurt. So did Manny's logic. "Are you joking? That's absurd, Sinatra. What's the real plan? Use my phone, call Weaver."

"Weaver? She can't help! We call Señora Weaver after I have them in custody."

"I should have left you in prison."

"Besides," said Manny, looking behind at the jump plane's cargo. "There's like a hundred parachutes in here. I'll wear one. Hit the gas."

"Hit the gas," she grumbled.

38

Manny found extra chutes in the aft lockers. He donned a harness and cinched the straps tight until his ribs screamed, making sure the webbing cocooned his firearms.

"We're too low for parachutes," she told him. "Even if you release immediately, you could still fracture your spine."

"I know this, Beck, I jumped in the Army. Better than nothing, though."

"This is not a thing. This is not something people do. Not even special ops groups transfer planes mid-flight."

"We're not going fast, Beck. You'll get close and there'll be no danger. If I fall, you tail them and call Weaver."

Each retreated into their thoughts as the King Air made up the distance on the Cessna. A high speed chase in slow motion. At a quarter mile out, Beck throttled back to 75%, matching the Cessna's velocity. Catalina was fifty yards below their feet.

"Two hundred knots," she said, eyeing their speed. "Fairly slow. At least the air won't kill you on impact."

Manny, hugging the co-pilot seat from behind, said, "They don't know we're here. Take us in."

Her stomach flip flopped. "This is asinine."

"No, it's charcuterie."

"Shut up, Sinatra." Her voice shook as the distance between planes shrunk. The red spine of the Cessna swelled from a miniature toy to life-size. The King Air wobbled and jumped as she lowered and corrected.

Manny threw wide the plane's jump door and the world rushed in. Order opened into chaos. The earth tilted below, hazy forest and farmland churning passed. Wind filled the cabin. Beck shouted and fought for control.

He grinned and spoke into the radio. "This is the most fun I've ever had, Beck. I'm glad you're here." He took the headset off, tossed it onto the co-pilot's chair, and braced himself on the exterior step. The wind ripped the loafer off his foot. Instantly gone.

"Damn it!"

"What?"

"Lost my shoe. An Allen Edmonds, made in Wisconsin."

"You're going to die, Sinatra," she said, reducing her altitude. Soon their turbulence increased, hitting the Cessna's prop wash.

Manny sat on the deck, rolled onto his stomach, and scooted out backwards. He lost the other shoe. Dangling into nothing, his feet kicked wildly until connecting with the port wheel.

"Stay away from their propeller!" he shouted. "And don't raise the landing gear!"

"Landing gear!" she said. "That's what I forgot. Whoops."

"I'll give a thump before I let go. *Te amo*, Beck!" He vanished out of sight.

She set her chin. That was the power of Manuel Martinez. His energy and confidence and momentum caught her up. She would do anything for him in that moment.

"Good luck, Sinatra," she muttered.

The wind snapped at him underneath the King Air. The twin propellers were tornadoes, slowly carving away his features. Only facing backwards could he open his eyes. His face hurt, his ribs hurt.

Beck did well. The Cessna wasn't far below. And beyond it, eternity.

He increased pressure with his fingers on the tire's axle stub. Released pressure with his knees and lowered his legs, searching. The wind pushed his body backwards, almost like a cape flapping.

This was as close as Beck dared get. And still the drop was too far. He felt the King Air kicking, flying through choppy atmosphere.

The Cessna was only a four-seater. The model with wings above the cabin instead of below, giving him a larger landing area. The cabin had windows in each direction, including aft. He and Beck had been lucky the piled cargo prevented them from being spotted.

His feet dangled above the Cessna's wings. Dangerously close to the propeller but he knew he couldn't fall forward.

Now, before he lost his nerve.

Such a bad idea.

He raised up to give the fuselage a solid whack, telling Beck he was letting go.

And he did.

Falling now. Windmilling. The air caught and hurled him backwards. Missing the wings entirely, landing on the tail, a thunderous impact, and sliding hard into the raised fin. The wind's pressure pinned him there. Adrenaline kept the worst of the pain away.

Beck felt the jolt of release. She pulled the yoke and arced from the Cessna, heart in her throat.

Sudden blue sky above Manny, the shadow gone.

The Cessna shuddered and wobbled. They saw him. The cockpit had windows in all directions but in the rear windshield he saw only the reflection of clouds above.

Hello Catalina. Wish I could see your face.

He couldn't get his breath. His harness was caught on the fin and he couldn't adjust his position.

The plane pitched upward and rolled to starboard. Pilot trying to dislodge him but his mass affected the slip stream current.

One hand holding tight, the other snaked under his harness. Grabbed the Glock's grip and tugged. Forced his eyes open against the wind. Kept the pistol near his chest to avoid swirling vicissitudes, aimed slightly down at the bottom of the rear windshield, and fired.

Two, three, four, five, six.

The glass cracked and splintered. Shards tinkling into his face. Rounds thudding directly into the cockpit controls. Broken shouting reached his ears. The engine uttered a peculiar whine.

He pressed the gun then directly into the tail and fired again.

Seven, eight.

Liquid spurted from the puckered bullet holes. Hot and thick. Oil? Gasoline? The engine whining again and now coughing.

Inside the cockpit, a gun fired.

He felt rather than heard a snapping near his ear, like an angry hornet. They were shooting at him, a sitting duck pinned against the fin.

Time to go—Cessna in her death throes.

He reached behind, grasped the drogue and yanked. The pilot chute caught.

As the sequence of straps and nylon hurled from his harness, he mused a more cautious man would've checked to ensure the chute was packed correctly.

Inside the cabin they shot at him again. But he was gone, nearly yanked out of the harness. Sky rushing down. Gasping now, dangling below a full canvas umbrella. The shattering noise of wind and engine vanished, replaced by immediate calm. The ground impact wouldn't be brutal— there had been no downward acceleration.

"Hah," he laughed and winced. "Asinine, Beck said. Never a doubt."

He drifted toward the vast green of Indian Mountain State Park. Far overhead, Beck's King Air kept pace with the Cessna.

39

Catalina's ears rang from gunshots, head between her knees. Cautiously she glanced at her brother—he was done shooting, now wrestling with the damaged controls.

She twisted to peer over her seat at the man retreating in the distance. Of course Manuel had found them. She could fool the FBI, sure, but some men are made from different stuff. He hadn't returned her calls or messages. Had he planned this?

In Spanish, she said, "Manuel looks good holding a gun, yes? But where did he come from?" She tilted her head to peer upwards through the window.

"Be quiet, little sister," said Rafael. "I need to think." He was a good pilot, hundreds of hours in the air over Honduras and Guatemala. He knew disaster when he saw it. "The aviation systems are ruined," he told her. The dash blinked and sparked, broken by bullets. "This plane is old enough I could fly without them, but..." He tapped a few dials operating on hydraulic pressure, not electronics. "We are losing oil and fuel both. The ignition will—"

The dash sparked and a small flame danced, visible inside the housing.

"We need to get on the ground. Right now," he said.

He flipped off the master switch and the fire went out.

Catalina nodded and she made a call. She spoke with the man on the other end, and asked her brother, "Where are we?"

"There," said Rafael, pointing at cultivated land. A flat cotton field. He pitched the Cessna sharply forward. The landing would be rough. "We land there. I don't know when we'll see flat land again."

"Where are we?" she asked again. "They need to get us."

"I don't know! Use the damned map on your phone. Near...I don't know. Near Tennessee."

She spoke into the phone again.

Rafael said, "Brace yourself, little sister."

Manny guided the chute down, aiming for a small clearing. He had no desire to get stuck in a treetop. Ground coming fast.

Before the forest enveloped him, he saw the Cessna dive. Heading to the earth for a crash landing not two miles distant.

He smiled to himself.

A reckoning.

The propeller seized short of the fields. Rafael fought to keep the Cessna level. As the landing gear skimmed the first trees, he made sure all systems were off.

They held hands.

The Cessna had decelerated to sixty knots when the first big oak nearly sheered off their starboard wing. Catalina and Rafael were hurled sideways against restraining harnesses. The forward momentum persisted but now the aircraft spun in a rotation. Smaller trees broke, the Cessna acting as a lawn mower blade. All windows shattered, tree branches reaching in. Glass perforating their faces. Metal screamed and the wing struts ripped free. The tumble finally ended at a thick pine, which caved the tail and dropped the smoking fuselage to the earth.

Rafael's head thundered. Catalina blinked away stars.

"We must go," he said. Words sounded slurred, like underwater. His door wouldn't open. Nor would hers. "There could be fire. Now!" He undid his safety straps and went forward, crawling through the rent windshield. No bones broken, though both were heavily scratched. He reached in for her and guided her out. Dropped down to the forest floor. Moved fifty yards away and sat to rest.

No fires. No explosion. Smoke curled into the sky.

Catalina closed her eyes, head in her hands.

Rafael seethed. This was the fault of one man.

42

Manny found them by following the smoke. His feet bled from the hike, barefoot. The Cessna cut an ugly gash through the forest, the wreckage resting at the base of a gentle rise, smoldering on old brown pine needles. Rafael had half of their luggage freed.

From behind a poplar Manny watched Catalina. Was she crying? He hardened his heart. Even now she was beautiful. Even now she was the girl from his youth.

He didn't want her in prison. But he didn't want her on that plane, flying back to wreck more lives, hers and others. He was torn.

They didn't hear his approach. These were not survivalists, not fighters. These were wealthy bureaucrats and spoiled terrorists, used to issuing orders from couches. Defending themselves an afterthought.

In Spanish, Manny called, "The trouble with foreign planes, the engines always die."

Catalina's head whipped around.

Rafael released the duffle bag he'd been tugging. He searched the ground for his pistol and lunged for it.

"Don't do it," said Manny. "You'll shoot your*self* before getting me."

Rafael held the revolver with two hands and fired toward Manny's voice, missing his tree by ten feet.

Manny called, "You're a crime boss, Rafael, not a fighter. If you make me, I'll kill you."

"Come out! Come out, you lying son of a bitch!"

"Manuel," shouted Catalina, backing toward the wreckage. "Please, we must go! Come with us!"

His head swam. He'd heard those words before. He felt woozy.

Rafael's hands were bloody and he side-stepped to get a better angle. Manny had only one bullet remaining in the Glock.

"Rafael, your money won't save you here. You are no killer. I could shoot you now," said Manny from behind his tree. "You aren't taking cover. You're exposed. You're like a stupid baby with that. Put the gun down."

"I'm not going to jail! Never again!" He fired. Closer this time, hitting the adjacent tree.

"Catalina. Tell him to drop it. Otherwise I kill him. I do one thing well in this world, Rafael, and this is it. You won't win."

"Manuel, please! We need you. *I* need you. Our men will be here soon, from the interstate, and we'll leave with them."

Their security crew would be following the plane, taking different routes in case the cars were pulled over. He needed to be gone before they arrived.

He said, "Your trick worked. You fooled the feds. Very clever."

"But we didn't trick you, Manuel. You are too smart. That is why we need you."

"No!" shouted Rafael. "We don't need this traitor. A traitor to his country, to his people. We are the García family. This man does not deserve us. Does not deserve *you*."

Manny chuckled, pivoting around the tree trunk, keeping an eye on Rafael. The fool still took no cover.

"Lucky I didn't kill you in the kitchen with a paddle, Fidel Arroyo."

"Manuel, we're going to Panama. *You* are going to Panama. I need you."

"No!" Rafael crab-walked to his right, aiming.

"Rafael!" shouted Manny, angry now. "This is why I don't give warnings. Put down the gun. You aren't a fighter, you aren't a killer. You are alive because of your sister!"

"I would rather be dead." Rafael fired again, kicking into the poplar trunk.

Manny stepped from cover. Kept stepping to his right. Brought the Glock up. "If you shoot again, so do I. You'll miss. I won't."

Rafael stood still. One eye screwed up, aiming.

Manny went behind another trunk. Circling, constant movement, carefully placing his feet. Gunsight fixed on Rafael's chest.

Rafael yanked the trigger, pulling his pistol off target as Manny had seen him do three times already. He missed, four feet too high.

Shaking his head, Manny said, "You're no fighter, Rafael. Bad decision."

"Manuel, no!"

Rafael charged him. Rich, powerful, attractive man tripping over maple roots, still holding the revolver.

Manny fired at a distance of seven feet. Caught his target between the eyes.

Rafael, dead before he hit the pine needles. His body slid face first down the gentle rise and stopped. Gunfire echoing among the trunks.

"Warnings never work." Manny experienced no sense of victory.

Catalina...

No outrage from her. No scream of grief. She rose from her crouch near the wreckage. Wiped her cheeks and went to her brother. She lowered to her knees. Took shuddering breaths. Used her fingertips to close his eyes, coming away crimson.

"The last brother I have left to bury," she said. Manny barely heard. "Death. It never stops fascinating me."

This is why you don't get on that plane.

It cost more than your soul.

Manny closed his eyes too. "I'm sorry Catalina."

A long silence. Even the birds and squirrels stayed respectful.

When he opened them again, Catalina had the revolver. She held it easier than her brother, in her right hand, arm straight. She raised to stand, the barrel three feet from Manny's face.

Manny dropped his Glock.

She said, "You still love me."

"I always will. I think."

"But..."

"But I'm not going to Panama. Or Honduras. Or anywhere else."

"I'm disappointed, Manuel." She'd changed in sixty seconds. From grieving sister and forlorn lover...to the type of person Manny chased for a living. "I could use you. You're the most dangerous man alive. Yet you refuse. Why, I wonder..."

She stepped forward. Barrel against his chest. Shoved her hand into his left pants pocket and felt nothing. Rooted next in his right. Tossed out his wallet, and came away with the photograph. Of the smiling woman.

"Of course." She laughed, a bitter mocking sound. She shook it. "So weak. Of course because of her, your precious *mama*."

Again his head swam. Just like on the tarmac, as a young man, she shook it at him.

"Your mama doesn't love you."

"Doesn't mean I don't love her. I choose the things I love."

"You feel it. I know you—you admitted it. Some days you don't want to wake up. Nothing we do matters in the long run. Does it, Manuel? That is why you cling to her."

"I am more than what I cling to, Catalina. I have to be. It keeps away the dark."

"*Nothing* keeps away the dark."

"You mean, money and power don't."

"And *she* does?" shouted Catalina. The heat of her breath reached his neck "You found her. I know you did. And?"

"And she's broken. Still lost."

"You think saving your mama makes you noble." A sneer.

"Makes me human."

"You won't give up on her," she said.

"Never."

"You gave up on *me*."

"No. You left. You both left."

"Poor Manuel." Her lips twisted, angry and mean. "All alone."

He stayed silent. She searched his eyes, bouncing back

and forth between them. Their gazes collided like rods breaking. He wouldn't beg. She knew it and she hated him for it.

"You aren't coming with me," she said.

"No."

"You'll stay here, in America. You get it, right? You get the symbolism, Manuel, you child. You foolish immature child. You want to be American so badly. You think you *are* America. You think by saving it you can save yourself."

He tried to reply—the words stuck. The truth often takes our breath.

She said, "This country can't love you back."

He was embarrassed at how thick and hot his words sounded. "It's not going anywhere. That's something."

"Poor Manny, clinging to his fat arrogant country. Hoping patriotism makes him whole. A boy pretending to be a man, playing hero. Think you can save America. Think you can save me, the lost girl."

"I'm a fool for the women I love."

"I'm not a girl who can be saved. I'm the girl America needs to be saved *from*."

He nodded. Grim. "I see that. Now."

"You should not have dropped your gun, Manuel."

"You shouldn't have picked yours up."

"No?" That excitement in her eyes. "I'm going to kill you, love me or not. Watch your life bleed out of you."

"Go ahead, Catalina."

"You think I won't."

"I think you *can't.*"

She laughed. A mocking sound. "You still underestimate me."

"No. My fault is, I overestimated you."

"Took you to my bed. And then killed you. Just like so many other men."

He didn't reply.

Her thumb drew the revolver's hammer drew back. Click.

She said, "Goodbye, Manuel."

She pulled the trigger. Click.

She pulled it again, harder this time, Click

Manny's heart fell. He was wrong—he predicted she wouldn't. Hell hath no fury...

"Empty," she said like she was dizzy. Threw the gun at him and missed. "You *knew?*"

"I always count. Rafael used six shots."

Her hands shook. Her voice shook, with sudden fear. "I'm not going to jail."

"I agree."

Her breath caught. She glanced at the Glock in the pine needles.

She said, "You wouldn't shoot me."

"Might be surprised. I'm not crazy about the way you speak of America."

"No! You won't shoot me. You love me. Let me go, Manuel."

He stepped on the Glock, pinning it under his toe.

"Let me go, Manuel, or when my men get here I'll send you straight to hell. First you and then your fat, lazy, arrogant country. Please!"

He reached under his arm for his .357 Smith & Wesson revolver, made in America, grasped, pulled, and shot her. The impact formed a triangle with her eyes. Her head snapped back and she fell like a tree, almost hitting her head on the broken wing.

"You should've stayed, Catalina. With me. We'd both

be different people now. But on the bright side..." He took a deep breath. And then another, filling his lungs until his ribs hurt. "...you're no longer on our most wanted list."

He stepped forward, boot touching her shoulder. He lowered the gun without looking at her and shot her twice more in the chest. Loud angry blasts.

Holstered the revolver.

Only then did he allow his heart to shatter.

Manny was sitting on the ground, leaning against the guard rail on the interstate when Weaver arrived at 9pm—he'd activated the GPS device in his belt and waited. He winced against the headlight, got up, and stamped his feet to restore circulation.

He slid into the back with Weaver, and he tossed a small leather satchel onto the empty driver seat. The Tesla piloted itself.

"You look like hell, Sinatra."

"Should see the other guy."

"Need a hospital?"

"It'll heal."

"You're barefoot. And bleeding. Should we stop at Walmart for flip-flops?"

"I would rather die."

She smiled. "Give me some good news."

"Plane went down a few miles west from here, in the state park." He handed her a phone. El Gato's phone. On screen was a map. "There. You'll find the wreckage. El Gato is dead. So is her brother, Rafael

García, also known as Fidel Arroyo and Ricardo Herrera."

On the way to Lonesome Pine airport, he filled her in on the details. The drive took forty-five minutes. She listened, asked only a few questions.

Noelle Beck waited for them in the dark parking lot, leaning against his Camaro. Keith the jumper had waited with her, listening to the forest hum with insects—he left when her ride arrived. Manny got out and surprised everyone, even himself, wrapping her into a hug.

"*Gracias*, Beck. For not dying."

Her voice was muffled against his shoulder. "You're welcome, Sinatra."

"How'd you get down?" He released.

A trace of pride in her smile. "An old friend in the Air Force talked me down. But we might get a bill for the landing gear I tore off. My impact was a little rough."

From the car, Weaver said, "Get in."

Manny took off his belt and Beck removed the storage card from the buckle. She inserted it into the car's built-in video screen—the world as seen from Manny's belt. Weaver fast forwarded to the jump from the King Air. Even on video, it took one's breath away.

"Good grief, Sinatra." On screen, the world spun out of focus.

Beck nodded. "That's what I said."

"Jumping out of airplanes isn't in the job description."

"Just an extra perk," said Manny.

"Too bad JFIC isn't officially recognized," muttered Weaver, watching the action. "You both deserve Shields of Bravery." She buzzed ahead to the confrontation at the Cessna wreckage. Manny closed his eyes and lowered his head, declining to watch. Weaver grunted when Manny shot Garcia. Both gasped when he shot Catalina. She released a long breath through her nose. "Well done. I know that was tough."

"But...why?" asked Beck.

"Catalina wouldn't go quietly. I knew she wouldn't, and her men were on the way. And I couldn't carry her for miles. And...she didn't want to go to jail. I had no good options."

On screen, Manny dragged Catalina and then Rafael to the wreckage. He went through their pockets and duffle bags, and used her finger to unlock the phone. Anything that looked worth saving, like memory sticks and passports, he shoved into a small leather satchel. He opened the fuel tank then, jamming a stick inside the valve to keep the gasoline spurting out. The picture went sideways and blurry as he crawled into the Cessna's ruined cabin, hunted and came out with a flare.

Beck leaned forward to watch, resting her chin in her hand.

On screen, Manny lit the flare. He walked to the far side of the plane, said, "Goodbye Catalina," tossed the flare near the spreading gasoline, turned his back, and walked away.

He'd gone twenty paces when the ground and trunks flashed a brilliant red. The microphone picked up the deep whump of combustion.

Weaver hit pause. "Why burn the bodies and plane?"

"She said her men were on the way. I believed her. They would be arriving before I could call for police or anyone else. So I burned it all."

"In case the luggage or cargo was valuable to them?"

"Right. I doubt her men will find anything. They

might bury the bodies or take the charred luggage, that's it."

Weaver said, "You two saved our ass, you know that? Prevented a lot of embarrassment. And probably more than a few jobs."

Manny didn't respond.

Saving the realm. Saving himself. Trying to become a man. Catalina's words would be hard to dislodge.

"Just doing our jobs, ma'am." Beck smiled. She looked exhausted. "I've always wanted to say that."

"I'll give Beck a ride home," said Manny.

"I need reports tomorrow. From both of you."

He grunted. "Paperwork."

"But after that, you two need a few days off. That's an order." She stepped out into the deserted Lonesome Pine parking lot and shook both their hands. "Thank you, Beck. Sinatra. The country owes you."

She returned, pulled the door closed and drove away.

Beck said, "A debt the country will never repay, right?"

"America can't love us back," said Manny and he got her door. "But that's not why I do it."

She fell asleep almost immediately on the drive home.

He squeezed her hand and didn't let go.

44

They reached Roanoke at two in the morning. Beck awake, barely, scanning her phone and yawning.

He braked to a stop in the middle of Campbell, downtown. Staring out his side window at a street bench.

He sighed.

She looked up. "Something wrong?"

"Your car is at my house?"

"Yes. My personal car."

"Drive my Camaro there. I need to take care of something." He got out, leaving the car idling.

She came around and got in the driver seat. "I might wreck this thing."

"Then you better flee to Canada."

She laughed. Made ready to close the door.

"Hey Beck."

"Yes?"

"*Gracias.* Thank you. For busting me out of jail."

"I got a feeling it might not be the last time." She grinned. It was a good look.

He said, "I changed my mind."

"About what?"

"You can come over more. To our house. I'll cook you dinner."

"I accept. Strictly platonic."

"Obviously."

She laughed.

He said, "You're a great American. Highest compliment I got."

"Sweet dreams, Sinatra. Manny. You earned them." She closed the door and purred down the street.

This late, the city was asleep. He walked halfway down Market Street. The old woman lay on her bench. OWS, Old Woman Sofia. Her favorite bench when the night was warm; he'd found her here before, a place the police didn't check. She was drunk. And maybe high but he could smell the alcohol.

He got his arms under her and lifted. His ribs hurt with the effort. But she weighed less than a hundred pounds and her place wasn't far, an apartment off Church.

He carried her and she mumbled. He let himself into the building with his key, carried her to the second floor, went into her unit, and laid her on the bed. The place felt empty—she might've sold some stuff, things he bought for her.

She smiled within her delirium.

"Helping an old woman," she said in Spanish. Peered blearily. "Cop. Bastard, police officer, leave me alone."

He went to the fridge and checked. Enough food for a couple days—cans of soup and cereal.

So tired. Eyes burning.

He went back to her small bedroom and laid a blanket over her.

"Let me see," she mumbled. "Let me see the photograph."

He took it out of his pocket. Unfolded it. Handed it to her.

She looked. Quickly her eyes filled with tears. "I was beautiful. A beautiful girl."

"Still are."

"No." She threw the photo. He grabbed it as it fluttered. "No. Not anymore. Long gone. That girl, I'm long gone."

He kissed her forehead. "I love you, *amá*."

"Don't know why, why you still call me that," she mumbled, eyes closed. "I haven't been your mother in a long time."

"But the only one I got."

She started to snore.

On the way out, he inspected her mail. Took the bills and shoved them in his pocket with the photograph.

Closed the door softly.

Took a moment to regroup.

45

At home, he climbed the stairs. Slow steps, enjoying the air conditioning and the smell of order.

He stopped in the hallway. On his left, Mackenzie's bedroom, the light still on. On his right, his own bedroom —dark. Unbearably empty, like a tomb, the bed a sarcophagus.

One day. Soon. Soon he could endure the loneliness.

But not tonight.

He went into Mackenzie's room. Mack lay on his bed, lamp burning, reading a book.

He asked, "Where are your shoes?"

"Barefoot, it's all the rage, Mack."

"I hope that's a joke. I don't understand millennials."

"We're the same age. You're up late, amigo."

"Just got in."

"Work?"

Mackenzie said, "Found a runaway girl hiding in a trailer in Floyd. Brought her home, because I am magnificent and magnanimous." He lowered the book he was reading, by Stephen Ambrose. Laid it across his chest. "Also, you do not look good."

"Yes I do."

"You look like mean guys hurt you."

"I look like charcuterie."

"You look like death."

"You wish you looked this good, *señor*." Manny lowered to his knees with a grunt. Pulled out his bedroll and inflated it. Stupid Chinese crap. Needed a new one.

"Rethinking your assignment to the black ops team?"

"No." Manny laid his head on his pillow, still fully dressed. His shirt smelled like prison and gun powder and interstate. Slid his two firearms and wallet under the bed. Tried to get comfortable—everything hurt. "I like saving the world."

"Not sure this world can be saved."

"Maybe nothing can be. But most fun I ever had, trying." He yawned. "And that's enough."

Manny fell fast asleep, dreamless.

EPILOGUE ONE

Special Agent Weaver sat at the renowned Round Robin bar in the Willard Hotel, two blocks removed from the White House, drinking a Leaves of Grass, lost in a ream of paperwork.

Douglas, the DEA's Director for Special Operations, stopped on his way to a table with a colleague. He leaned next to her, cleared this throat, and spoke softly.

"I read the report last night. JFIC hit a home run. Nice work, Weaver."

She smiled to herself.

He asked, "You'll use Sinatra again?"

With her pen, she indicated the paperwork and her iPad. "Yes. Maybe even sooner than he'd like."

EPILOGUE TWO

Catalina García fell, the bullet snapping her head back. So shocked she didn't feel the impact with the earth. Manuel's words barely registered...

"You should've stayed, Catalina. With me. We'd both be different people now. But on the bright side..." Manuel took a deep breath. "...you're no longer on our most wanted list."

He stepped forward, boot touching her shoulder. He lowered the gun and shot her twice more in the chest. Loud angry blasts. She tried to scream but the impacts drove her breath away.

For several minutes she couldn't move. Terror overrode her systems. The bullet in her brain. The two in her chest, her lungs, her heart. She could *feel* them. Had she been ten years older, the fear alone might've caused a cardiac episode. She'd never been so afraid.

Nor so surprised to be alive. But how...how could that be? Her head throbbed. Her chest burned.

Eventually her heart slowed. Her ears ceased thundering. Logic returned in lurches. She was alive.

She couldn't *feel* the bullets, that was her imagination, her horror.

Manuel was on the far side of the plane, working.

Gingerly she reached to her forehead. Found the impact. Her fingers came away with...dried blood? No...it was...

Wax. He'd shot her with wax bullets! She felt her chest. Two other wax imprints.

Why? Why would he...

He didn't believe in warnings.

He came back around and she played dead. She didn't understand why, though. He treated her like a corpse even though he knew she wasn't. He grabbed her feet and roughly hauled her next to the wreckage. Letting her feet drop onto the wing.

He was wearing a wire, she bet. Or being watched by satellite, some form of surveillance.

You're no longer on our most wanted list.

He's letting me go.

But they both had to play their parts.

Through slitted eyelids, she watched him—he wasn't playing nice. He took her passports, her papers, her data sticks, her credit cards, and even used her finger to unlock her phone. His propriety galled her.

One of Central America's foremost troublemakers, defanged and stranded, and she could only watch.

A few minutes later, he emerged from the cabin and went to the far side. Out of eyesight.

"Goodbye Catalina," he said.

Her cue. She turned and crawled. Away from the fuselage, away from the smell of gasoline, away from Manuel.

She crawled up the rise through pine needles as the

plane caught. Hid behind a tree and watched as he walked away.

Leaving me. Not looking back. Taking everything I need to leave the country.

Giving me a new start.

I'm a fool for the women I love, he said.

Alone, she watched the plane burn. She watched her brother burn. Hundreds of thousands in cash on board, she watched it burn.

She watched. And wondered.

Wondered what to do now.

Wondered about her past. Her future.

And wondered about Manuel Martinez.

CLICK HERE to read the next Sinatra thriller!

AUTHOR'S NOTE

I hope you enjoyed reading *The Supremacy License.*

(You did)

The New York Times called it, "A shot of energy! Action packed, the thriller of the year!"

(They did not write that.)

(I made it up.)

When I was building the story around Manny, I envisioned him as an American James Bond, plus a little John Wick. This was my first thriller novel and I enjoyed it so much I'm going to write more (I usually write mysteries). Maybe 50% mystery, 50% thriller.

Here are overly simplified definitions of each:

Mystery = bad thing happens at the beginning, but who did it?

Thriller = bad thing will happen at the end, but can the hero prevent it at great personal cost?

I like stories without filler. Stories you can read in two days, hard to put down, lots of dialogue. If you like them too, I'm going to be your favorite writer for the next twenty years.

.   .   .

I'M an independent author without the backing or resources of a massive publisher. I rely on word-of-mouth and Amazon reviews to thrive. If you're so inclined, leaving a review (good or bad) helps a lot.

PREVIEW OF BOOK TWO

Chapter One

Manny Martinez reached sixty miles per hour in a thirty-five on Patterson Avenue. His Camaro was accelerating in increments without permission, the engine eager and the driver's mind wandering.

"When I worked homicide in Richmond," said the guy riding in the back seat, and he paused to yawn. "We didn't get up this early, sir."

Manny glared in the rearview...

He'd forgotten the guy's name again. The kid was new.

"You're a marshal now, amigo," said Manny. "Maybe. America gives you the keys to freedom, you get up early."

"Maybe?" New Guy looked a little like Peter Parker on steroids. A baby. He did his best not to stare at the back of Manny Martinez's head. *The* Manny Martinez. "Sir? *Maybe* I'm a marshal?"

"There's a trial period or something, right?"

"No, sir, I'm a full-time red-blooded deputy marshal as of last week. Like you. I got the shirt to prove it."

"They give those shirts to anyone."

Collin Parks rode shotgun; he often did with Manny the last two years. From this angle, Manny thought his cauliflower ears unbearable. Collin tilted his head to address the backseat. "Don't listen to Manny, Boone. Wear the shirt with pride. And we don't all get up this early. Just our resident crazy-ass Puerto Rican, Captain America himself."

Boone! That was it. Boone.

Boone chuckled. "Our Captain America is Puerto Rican?"

"Nothing more American than a Puerto Rican." Manny jerked a thumb at himself. "And we're up early to catch this guy while he's asleep. Fewer problems that way. Usually I like a good fight, but maybe we should get this guy napping."

"Why's that, sir?" New Guy scanned his iPad, the target's dossier on screen.

Manny liked being called *sir*.

"This guy, his name's Donald. Donald is a former MMA fighter," said Collin Parks. He rubbed his eyes and blinked against the late summer sun peeking through trees. "Two hundred and fifty pounds. He's a Neo Nazi, hates everyone. And Manny's scared of him."

"*Scared?* I beat him before, amigo."

Collin kept talking over his shoulder. "Two years ago we're sent to bring Donald in for battery. Catch him at a bar and he's drunk. Watching a football game or something, and this guy is big. I mean, he looks bigger'n two-fifty. And Manny can't help himself—he sees a challenge.

He wants this guy to bolt or fight or something. Cause Manny's an ass."

Manny snorted. "Word you're searching for is hero."

"Anyway, Manny goes to cuff him, right at the bar. Takes his time. A little rough on the guy's shoulder. Makes fun of the guy's Neo Nazi tattoos. And Donald decides to resist. He flips out. Catches Manny off guard."

"I was giving him a head start."

"Donald whacks Manny good, and he's wearing one of those watches. You know the kind, big fat watch, looks stupid. The watch rips Manny's eyebrow off, or at least half of it. I got my stun gun out, ready to drop him, but Manny wants to do it the old-fashioned way. Fights the guy, middle of All Sports. Came away looking like ground beef, and that's why he's scared of Donald."

"Who won the fight? Did I win? Cause I thought I won."

Collin said, "Then why're we catching Donald sleeping this early, Manny? Cause you remember last time. And you're getting older."

"He's four weight classes above me. I do not feel *age*; I feel…prudence." Manny smiled—prudence. That was good.

He turned right on 21st Street and braked in front of a yellow one-story house. The carport had caved in and was used as a lean-to shed for bikes and rusted grills. The small front porch needed replacing and the screen door hung askance, the bottom hinges gone.

The three men got out of the Camaro and New Guy asked, "What's this place?"

"My favorite girl," said Manny. "She's an informant named Kelsey. I heard she knows where Donald is. I ask politely and then we go get him. Wait here."

He shrugged into a khaki sports jacket and fastened the top button and walked up the cracked sidewalk. Boone glanced down at his cargo khakis and blue U.S. Marshal shirt—Collin Parks was dressed the same— and wondered what rules of dress code he'd missed.

Manny Martinez bordered on being an urban legend in the Richmond office. A larger than life character the size of Paul Bunyan. Or Wyatt Earp. While the stories couldn't all be true, Boone had to admit the minor details were accurate so far—fast paced, well dressed, and the glistening hair.

Manny reached the front porch and raised a fist to knock.

On the interior side of the door, Donald the Neo Nazi watched him through the peephole. In his hands he held a cheap Stevens shotgun...

CLICK HERE to begin the next Sinatra book today!

Made in the USA
Middletown, DE
11 July 2021